PENGUIN BOOKS

MIKE AT WRYKYN

P. G. Wodehouse was born in Guildford in 1881 and educated at Dulwich College. After working for the Hong Kong and Shanghai Bank for two years, he left to earn his living as a journalist and storywriter, writing the 'By the Way' column in the old *Globe*. He also contributed a series of school stories to a magazine for boys, the *Captain*, in one of which Psmith made his first appearance. Going to America before the First World War, he sold a serial to the *Saturday Evening Post*, and for the next twenty-five years almost all his books appeared first in this magazine. He was part author and writer of the lyrics of eighteen musical comedies, including *Kissing Time*. He married in 1914 and in 1955 took American citizenship. He wrote over ninety books, and his work has won world-wide acclaim, having been translated into many languages. *The Times* hailed him as a 'comic genius recognized in his lifetime as a classic and an old master of farce'.

P. G. Wodehouse said, 'I believe there are two ways of writing novels. One is mine, making a sort of musical comedy without music and ignoring real life altogether; the other is going right deep down into life and not caring a damn . . .' He was created a Knight of the British Empire in the New Year's Honours List in 1975. In a BBC interview he said that he had no ambitions left now that he had been knighted and there was a waxwork of him in Madame Tussaud's. He died on St Valentine's Day in 1975 at the age of ninety-three.

D1323055

MIKE AT WRYKYN

P. G. WODEHOUSE

PENGUIN BOOKS

PENGUIN BOOKS

Published by the Penguin Group
Penguin Books Ltd, 27 Wrights Lane, London W8 5TZ, England
Viking Penguin, a division of Penguin Books USA Inc.
375 Hudson Street, New York, New York 10014, USA
Penguin Books Australia Ltd, Ringwood, Victoria, Australia
Penguin Books Canada Ltd, 2801 John Street, Markham, Ontario, Canada L3R 1B4
Penguin Books (NZ) Ltd, 182–190 Wairau Road, Auckland 10, New Zealand

Penguin Books Ltd, Registered Offices: Harmondsworth, Middlesex, England

First published as *Mike* by A. & C. Black 1909
Revised edition published in two parts as *Mike at Wrykyn* and *Mike and Psmith*
by Herbert Jenkins 1953
Mike at Wrykyn published in Penguin Books 1990
3 5 7 9 10 8 6 4 2

Copyright 1909, 1953 by P. G. Wodehouse
All rights reserved

Printed in England by Clays Ltd, St Ives plc

Except in the United States of America,
this book is sold subject to the condition
that it shall not, by way of trade or otherwise,
be lent, re-sold, hired out, or otherwise circulated
without the publisher's prior consent in any form of
binding or cover other than that in which it is
published and without a similar condition
including this condition being imposed
on the subsequent purchaser

CONTENTS

CONTENTS

CHAPTER I

MIKE

IT was a morning in the middle of April, and the Jackson family were consequently breakfasting in comparative silence. The cricket season had not begun, and except during the cricket season they were in the habit of devoting their powerful minds at breakfast almost exclusively to the task of victualling against the labours of the day. In May, June, July, and August the silence was broken. The three grown-up Jacksons played regularly in first-class cricket, and there was always keen competition among their brothers and sisters for the copy of the *Sportsman* which was to be found on the hall table with the letters. Whoever got it usually gloated over it in silence till urged wrathfully by the multitude to let them know what had happened; when it would appear that Joe had notched his seventh century, or that Reggie had been run out when he was just getting set, or, as sometimes occurred, that that ass Frank had dropped Sheppard or May in the slips before he had scored, with the result that the spared expert had made a couple of hundred and was still going strong.

In such a case the criticisms of the family circle, particularly of the smaller Jackson sisters, were so breezy and unrestrained that Mrs. Jackson felt it necessary to apply the closure. Indeed, Marjory Jackson, aged fourteen, had on three separate occasions been fined pudding at lunch for her caustic comments on the batting of her brother Reggie in important fixtures. Cricket was a tradition in the family, and the ladies were resolved that it should not be their fault if the standard was not kept up.

7

On this particular morning silence reigned. A deep gasp from some small Jackson, wrestling with bread-and-milk, and an occasional remark from Mr. Jackson on the letters he was reading, alone broke it.

"Mike's late again," said Mrs. Jackson plaintively, at last.

"He's getting up," said Marjory. "I went in to see what he was doing, and he was asleep. "So," she added with a satanic chuckle, "I squeezed a sponge over him. He swallowed an awful lot, and then he woke up, and tried to catch me, so he's certain to be down soon."

"Marjory!"

"Well, he was on his back with his mouth wide open, so I had to. He was snoring like anything."

"You might have choked him."

"I did," said Marjory with satisfaction. "Jam, please, Phyllis, you pig."

Mr. Jackson looked up.

"Mike will have to be more punctual when he goes to Wrykyn," he said.

"Oh, Father, is Mike going to Wrykyn?" asked Marjory. "When?"

"Next term," said Mr. Jackson. "I've just heard from Mr. Wain," he added across the table to Mrs. Jackson. "The house is full, but he is turning a small room into an extra dormitory, so he can take Mike after all."

The first comment on this momentous piece of news came from Bob Jackson. Bob was eighteen. The following term would be his last at Wrykyn, and, having won through so far without the infliction of a small brother, he disliked the prospect of not being allowed to finish as he had begun.

"I say!" he said. "What?"

"He ought to have gone before," said Mr. Jackson. "He's nearly fifteen. Much too old for that private school. He has had it all his own way there, and it isn't good for him."

"He's got cheek enough for ten," agreed Bob.

"Wrykyn will do him a world of good."

"We aren't in the same house. That's one comfort."

Bob was in Donaldson's. It softened the blow to a certain extent that Mike should be going to Wain's. He had the same feeling for Mike that most boys of eighteen have for their fifteen-year-old brothers. He was fond of him in the abstract, but preferred him at a distance.

Marjory gave tongue again. She had rescued the jam from Phyllis, who had shown signs of finishing it, and was now at liberty to turn her mind to less pressing matters. Mike was her special ally, and anything that affected his fortunes affected her.

"Hooray! Mike's going to Wrykyn. I bet he gets into the first eleven his first term."

"Considering there are eight old colours left," said Bob loftily, "besides heaps of last year's seconds, it's hardly likely that a kid like Mike'll get a look in. He might get his third, if he sweats."

The aspersion stung Marjory.

"I bet he gets in before you, anyway," she said.

Bob disdained to reply. He was among those heaps of last year's seconds to whom he had referred. He was a sound bat, though lacking the brilliance of his elder brothers, and he fancied that his cap was a certainty this season. Last year he had been tried once or twice. This year it should be all right.

Mrs. Jackson intervened.

"Go on with your breakfast, Marjory," she said. "You mustn't say 'I bet' so much."

Marjory bit off a section of her slice of bread-and-jam.

"Anyhow, I bet he does," she muttered truculently through it.

There was a sound of footsteps in the passage outside. The door opened, and the missing member of the family appeared. Mike Jackson was tall for his age. His figure was thin and wiry. His arms and legs looked a shade too long for his body. He was evidently going to be very tall some day. In face, he was curiously like his brother Joe, whose appearance is familiar to everyone who takes an interest in first-class cricket. The resemblance was even more marked on the cricket field. Mike had Joe's batting style to the last detail. He was a pocket edition of his century-making brother. "Hullo," he said, "sorry I'm late."

This was mere custom. He had made the same remark nearly every morning since the beginning of the holidays.

"All right, Marjory, you little beast," was his reference to the sponge incident.

His third remark was of a practical nature.

"I say, what's under that dish?"

"Mike," began Mr. Jackson—this again was custom—"you really must learn to be more punctual——"

He was interrupted by a chorus.

"Mike, you're going to Wrykyn next term," shouted Marjory.

"Mike, Father's just had a letter to say you're going to Wrykyn next term." From Phyllis.

"Mike, you're going to Wrykyn." From Ella.

Gladys Maud Evangeline, aged three, obliged with a solo of her own composition, in six-eight time, as follows: "Mike Wryky. Mike Wryky. Mike Wryke Wryke Wryke Mike Wryke Wryke Mike Wryke Mike Wryke."

"Oh, put a green baize cloth over that kid, somebody," groaned Bob.

Whereat Gladys Maud, having fixed him with a chilly stare for some seconds, suddenly drew a long breath, and squealed deafeningly for more milk.

Mike looked round the table. It was a great moment. He rose to it with the utmost dignity.

"Good," he said. "I say, what's under that dish?"

After breakfast, Mike and Marjory went off together to the meadow at the end of the garden. Saunders, the professional, assisted by the gardener's boy, was engaged in putting up the net. Mr. Jackson believed in private coaching; and every spring since Joe, the eldest of the family, had been able to use a bat a man had come down from the Oval to teach him the best way to do so. Each of the boys in turn had passed from spectators to active participants in the net practice in the meadow. For several years now Saunders had been the chosen man, and his attitude towards the Jacksons was that of the Faithful Old Retainer in melodrama. Mike was his special favourite. He felt that in him he had material of the finest order to work upon. There was nothing the matter with Bob. In Bob he would turn out a good, sound article. Bob would be a Blue in his third or fourth year, and probably a creditable performer among the rank and file of a county team later on. But he was not a cricket genius, like Mike. Saunders would lie awake at night sometimes thinking of the possibilities that were in Mike. The strength could only come with years, but the style was there already. Joe's style, with improvements.

Mike put on his pads; and Marjory walked with the professional to the bowling crease.

"Mike's going to Wrykyn next term, Saunders," she said. "All the boys were there, you know. So was Father, ages ago."

"Is he, miss? I was thinking he would be soon."

"Do you think he'll get into the school team?"

"School team, miss! Master Mike get into a school team! He'll be playing for England in another eight years. That's what he'll be playing for."

"Yes, but I meant next term. It would be a record if he did. Even Joe only got in after he'd been at school two years. Don't you think he might, Saunders? He's awfully good, isn't he? He's better than Bob, isn't he? And Bob's almost certain to get in this term."

Saunders looked a little doubtful.

"Next term!" he said. "Well, you see, miss, it's this way. It's all there, in a manner of speaking, with Master Mike. He's got as much style as Mr. Joe's got, every bit. The whole thing is, you see, miss, you get these young

11

gentlemen of eighteen, and nineteen perhaps, and it stands to reason they're stronger. There's a young gentleman, perhaps, doesn't know as much about what I call real playing as Master Mike's forgotten; but then he can hit 'em harder when he does hit 'em, and that's where the runs come in. They aren't going to play Master Mike because he'll be in the England team when he leaves school. They'll give a cap to somebody that can make a few then and there."

"But Mike's jolly strong."

"Ah, I'm not saying it mightn't be, miss. I was only saying don't count on it, so you won't be disappointed if it doesn't happen. It's quite likely that it will, only all I say is don't count on it. I only hope that they won't knock all the style out of him before they're done with him. You know these school professionals, miss."

"No, I don't, Saunders. What are they like?"

"Well, there's too much of the come-right-out-at-everything about 'em for my taste. Seem to think playing forward the alpha and omugger of batting. They'll make him pat balls back to the bowler which he'd cut for twos and threes if he was left to himself. Still, we'll hope for the best, miss. Ready, Master Mike? Play."

As Saunders had said, it was all there. Of Mike's style there could be no doubt. Today, too, he was playing more strongly than usual. Marjory had to run to the end of the meadow to fetch one straight drive. "He hit that hard enough, didn't he, Saunders?" she asked, as she returned the ball.

"If he could keep on doing ones like that, miss," said the professional, "they'd have him in the team before you could say knife."

Marjory sat down again beside the net, and watched more hopefully.

CHAPTER II

THE JOURNEY DOWN

THE seeing off of Mike on the last day of the holidays was an imposing spectacle, a sort of pageant. Going to a public school, especially at the beginning of the summer term, is no great hardship, more particularly when the departing hero has a brother on the verge of the school eleven and three other brothers playing for counties; and Mike seemed in no way disturbed by the prospect. Mothers, however, to the end of time will foster a secret fear that their sons will be bullied at a big school, and Mrs. Jackson's anxious look lent a fine solemnity to the proceedings.

And as Marjory, Phyllis, and Ella invariably broke down when the time of separation arrived, and made no exception to their rule on the present occasion, a suitable gloom was the keynote of the gathering. Mr. Jackson seemed to bear the parting with fortitude, as did Mike's Uncle John (providentially roped in at the eleventh hour on his way to Scotland, in time to come down with a handsome tip). To their coarse-fibred minds there was nothing pathetic or tragic about the affair at all. Among others present might have been noticed Saunders, practising late cuts rather coyly with a walking-stick in the background; the village idiot, who had rolled up on the chance of a tip; Gladys Maud Evangeline's nurse, smiling vaguely; and Gladys Maud Evangeline herself, frankly bored with the whole business.

The train gathered speed. The air was full of last messages. Gladys Maud cried, because she had taken a sudden dislike to the village idiot; and Mike settled himself in his corner and opened a magazine.

He was alone in the carriage. Bob, who had been spending the last week of the holidays with an aunt further down the line, was to board the train at East Wobsley, and the brothers were to make a state entry into Wrykyn together. Meanwhile, Mike was left to his milk chocolate, his magazines, and his reflections.

The latter were not numerous, nor profound. He was excited. He had been petitioning the home authorities for the past year to be allowed to leave his prep. school and go to Wrykyn, and now the thing had come about. He wondered what sort of a house Wain's was, and whether they had any chance of the cricket cup. According to Bob they had no earthly; but then Bob only recognized one house, Donaldson's. He wondered if Bob would get his first eleven cap this year, and if he himself were likely to do anything at cricket. Marjory had faithfully reported every word Saunders had said on the subject, but Bob had been so careful to point out his insignificance when compared with the humblest Wrykynian that the professional's glowing prophecies had not had much effect. It might be true that some day he would play for England, but just at present he felt he would exchange his place in the team for one in the Wrykyn third eleven. A sort of mist enveloped everything Wrykynian. It seemed almost hopeless to try and compete with these unknown experts. On the other hand, there was Bob. Bob, by all accounts, was on the verge of the first eleven, and he was nothing special.

While he was engaged on these reflections, the train drew up at a small station. Opposite the door of Mike's compartment was standing a boy of about Mike's size, though evidently some years older. He had a sharp face, with rather a prominent nose; and a pair of pince-nez gave him a supercilious look. He wore a bowler hat, and carried a small portmanteau.

He opened the door, and took the seat opposite to Mike,

whom he scrutinized for a moment rather after the fashion of a naturalist examining some new and unpleasant variety of beetle. He seemed about to make some remark, but, instead, got up and looked through the open window.

"Where's that porter?" Mike heard him say.

The porter came skimming down the platform at that moment.

"Porter."

"Sir?"

"Are those trunks of mine in all right?"

"Yes, sir."

"Because, you know, there'll be a frightful row if any of them get lost."

"No chance of that, sir."

"Here you are, then."

"Thank you, sir."

The youth drew his head and shoulders in, stared at Mike again, and finally sat down. Mike noticed that he had nothing to read, and wondered if he wanted anything; but he did not feel equal to offering him one of his magazines. He did not like the looks of him particularly. Judging by appearances, he seemed to have side enough for three. If he wanted a magazine, thought Mike, let him ask for it.

The other made no overtures, and at the next stop got out. That explained his magazineless condition. He was only travelling a short way.

"Good business," said Mike to himself. He had all the Englishman's love of a carriage to himself.

The train was just moving out of the station when his eye was suddenly caught by the stranger's bag, lying snugly in the rack.

And here, I regret to say, Mike acted from the best motives, which is always fatal.

He realized in an instant what had happened. The fellow had forgotten his bag.

Mike had not been greatly fascinated by the stranger's looks; but, after all, the most supercilious person on earth has a right to his own property. Besides, he might have been quite a nice fellow when you got to know him. Anyhow, the bag had better be returned at once. The train was already moving quite fast, and Mike's compartment was nearing the end of the platform.

He snatched the bag from the rack and hurled it out of the window. (Porter Robinson, who happened to be in the line of fire, escaped with a flesh wound.) Then he sat down again with the inward glow of satisfaction which comes to one when one has risen successfully to a sudden emergency.

The glow lasted till the next stoppage, which did not occur for a good many miles. Then it ceased abruptly, for the train had scarcely come to a standstill when the opening above the door was darkened by a head and shoulders. The head was surmounted by a bowler, and a pair of pince-nez gleamed from the shadow.

"Hullo, I say," said the stranger. "Have you changed carriages, or what?"

"No," said Mike.

"Then, where's my bag?"

Life teems with embarrassing situations. This was one of them.

"The fact is," said Mike, "I chucked it out."

"Chucked it out! What do you mean? When?"

"At the last station."

The guard blew his whistle, and the other jumped into the carriage.

"I thought you'd got out there for good," explained Mike. "I'm awfully sorry."

"Where *is* the bag?"

"On the platform at the last station. It hit a porter."

Against his will, for he wished to treat the matter with fitting solemnity, Mike grinned at the recollection. The look on Porter Robinson's face as the bag took him in the small of the back had been funny, though not intentionally so.

The bereaved owner disapproved of this levity; and said as much.

"Don't *grin*, you little beast," he shouted. "There's nothing to laugh at. You go chucking bags that don't belong to you out of the window, and then you have the frightful cheek to grin about it."

"It wasn't that," said Mike hurriedly. "Only the porter looked awfully funny when it hit him."

"Dash the porter! What's going to happen about my bag? I can't get out for half a second to buy a magazine without your flinging my things about the platform. What you want is a sound kicking."

The situation was becoming difficult. But fortunately at this moment the train stopped once again; and, looking out of the window, Mike saw a board with East Wobsley upon it in large letters. A moment later Bob's head appeared in the doorway.

"Hullo, there you are," said Bob.

His eye fell upon Mike's companion.

"Hullo, Gazeka!" he exclaimed. "Where did you spring from? Do you know my brother? He's coming to Wrykyn this term. By the way, rather lucky you've met. He's in your house. Firby-Smith's head of Wain's, Mike."

Mike gathered that Gazeka and Firby-Smith were one and the same person. He grinned again. Firby-Smith continued to look ruffled, though not aggressive.

"Oh, are you in Wain's?" he said.

"I say, Bob," said Mike, "I've made rather an ass of myself."

"Naturally."

"I mean, what happened was this. I chucked Firby-Smith's bag out of the window, thinking he'd got out, only he hadn't really, and it's at a station miles back."

"You're a bit of a rotter, aren't you? Had it got your name and address on it, Gazeka?"

"Yes."

"Oh, then it's certain to be all right. It's bound to

17

turn up some time. They'll send it on by the next train, and you'll get it either tonight or tomorrow."

"Frightful nuisance, all the same. Lots of things in it I wanted."

"Oh, never mind, it's all right. I say, what have you been doing in the holidays? I didn't know you lived on this line at all."

From this point onwards Mike was out of the conversation altogether. Bob and Firby-Smith talked of Wrykyn, discussing events of the previous term of which Mike had never heard. Names came into their conversation which were entirely new to him. He realized that school politics were being talked, and that contributions from him to the dialogue were not required. He took up his magazine again, listening the while. They were discussing Wain's now. The name Wyatt cropped up with some frequency. Wyatt was apparently something of a character. Mention was made of rows in which he had played a part in the past.

"It must be pretty rotten for him," said Bob. "He and Wain never get on very well, and yet they have to be together, holidays as well as term. Pretty bad having a step-father at all—I shouldn't care to—and when your house-master and your step-father are the same man, it's a bit thick."

"Frightful," agreed Firby-Smith.

"I swear, if I were in Wyatt's place, I should rag about like anything. It isn't as if he'd anything to look forward to when he leaves. He told me last term that Wain had got a nomination for him in some beastly bank, and that he was going into it directly after the end of this term. Rather rough on a chap like Wyatt. Good cricketer and footballer, I mean, and all that sort of thing. It's just the sort of life he'll hate most. Hullo, here we are."

Mike looked out of the window. It was Wrykyn at last.

CHAPTER III

MIKE FINDS A FRIENDLY NATIVE

MIKE was surprised to find, on alighting, that the platform was entirely free from Wrykynians. In all the stories he had read the whole school came back by the same train, and, having smashed in one another's hats and chaffed the porters, made their way to the school buildings in a solid column. But here they were alone.

A remark of Bob's to Firby-Smith explained this. "Can't make out why none of the fellows came back by this train," he said. "Heaps of them must come by this line, and it's the only Christian train they run."

"Don't want to get here before the last minute they can possibly manage. Silly idea. I suppose they think there'd be nothing to do."

"What shall *we* do?" said Bob. "Come and have some tea at Cook's?"

"All right."

Bob looked at Mike. There was no disguising the fact that he would be in the way; but how convey this fact delicately to him?

"Look here, Mike," he said, with a happy inspiration, "Firby-Smith and I are just going to get some tea. I think you'd better nip up to the school. Probably Wain will want to see you, and tell you all about things, which is your dorm. and so on. See you later," he concluded airily. "Anyone'll tell you the way to the school. Go straight on. They'll send your luggage on later. So long." And his sole prop in this world of strangers departed, leaving him to find his way for himself.

There is no subject on which opinions differ so widely as this matter of finding the way to a place. To the man who knows, it is simplicity itself. Probably he really does imagine that he goes straight on, ignoring the fact that for him the choice of three roads, all more or less straight, has no perplexities. The man who does not know feels as if he were in a maze.

Mike started out boldly, and lost his way. Go in which direction he would, he always seemed to arrive at a square with a fountain and an equestrian statue in its centre. On the fourth repetition of this feat he stopped in a disheartened way, and looked about him. He was beginning to feel bitter towards Bob. The chap might at least have shown him where to get some tea.

At this moment a ray of hope shone through the gloom. Crossing the square was a short, thick-set figure clad in grey flannel trousers, a blue blazer, and a straw hat with a coloured band. Plainly a Wrykynian. Mike made for him.

"Can you tell me the way to the school, please," he said.

"Oh, you're going to the school," said the other. He had a pleasant, square-jawed face, reminiscent of a good-tempered bulldog, and a pair of very deep-set grey eyes which somehow put Mike at his ease. There was something singularly cool and genial about them. He felt that they saw the humour in things, and that their owner was a person who liked most people and whom most people liked.

"You look rather lost," said the stranger. "Been hunting for it long?"

"Yes," said Mike.

"Which house do you want?"

"Wain's."

"Wain's? Then you've come to the right man this time. What I don't know about Wain's isn't worth knowing."

"Are you there, too?"

"Am I not! Term *and* holidays. There's no close season for me."

"Oh, are you Wyatt, then?" asked Mike.

"Hullo, this is fame. How did you know my name, as the ass in the detective story always says to the detective, who's seen it in the lining of his hat? Who's been talking about me?"

"I heard my brother saying something about you in the train."

"Who's your brother?"

"Jackson. He's in Donaldson's."

"I know. A stout fellow. So you're the newest make of Jackson, latest model, with all the modern improvements? Are there any more of you?"

"Not brothers," said Mike.

"Pity. You can't quite raise a team, then? Are you a sort of young Compton, too?"

"I played a bit at my last school. Only a kids' school, you know," added Mike modestly.

"Make any runs? What was your best score?"

"Hundred and twenty-three," said Mike awkwardly. "It was only against kids, you know." He was in terror lest he should seem to be bragging.

"That's pretty useful. Any more centuries?"

"Yes," said Mike, shuffling.

"How many?"

"Seven altogether. You know, it was really awfully rotten bowling. And I was a good bit bigger than most of the chaps there. And my father always has a pro down in the Easter holidays, which gave me a bit of an advantage."

"All the same, seven centuries isn't so dusty against any bowling. We shall want some batting in the house this term. Look here, I was just going to have some tea. You come along, too."

"Oh, thanks awfully," said Mike. "My brother and Firby-Smith have gone to a place called Cook's."

"The old Gazeka? I didn't know he lived in your part of the world. He's head of Wain's."

"Yes, I know," said Mike. "Why is he called Gazeka?" he asked after a pause.

"Don't you think he looks like one? What did you think of him?"

"I didn't speak to him much," said Mike cautiously. It is always delicate work answering a question like this unless one has some sort of an inkling as to the views of the questioner.

"He's all right," said Wyatt, answering for himself. "He's got a habit of talking to one as if he were a prince of the blood, but that's his misfortune. We all have our troubles. That's his. Let's go in here. It's too far to sweat to Cooks."

It was about a mile from the teashop to the school. Mike's first impression on arriving at the school grounds was of his smallness and insignificance. Everything looked so big—the buildings, the grounds, everything. He felt out of the picture. He was glad that he had met Wyatt. To make his entrance into this strange land alone would have been more of an ordeal than he would have cared to face.

"That's Wain's," said Wyatt, pointing to one of half a dozen large houses which lined the road on the south side of the cricket field. Mike followed his finger, and took in the size of his new home.

"I say, it's jolly big," he said. "How many fellows are there in it?"

"Thirty-one this term, I believe."

"That's more than there were at King-Hall's."

"What's King-Hall's?"

"The prep. school I was at. At Emsworth."

Emsworth seemed very remote and unreal to him as he spoke.

They skirted the cricket field, walking along the path that divided the two terraces. The Wrykyn playing-fields were formed of a series of huge steps, cut out of the hill. At the top of the hill came the school. On the first terrace was a sort of informal practice ground, where, though no games were played on it, there was a good deal of punting and drop-kicking in the winter and fielding-practice in the summer. The next terrace was the biggest of all, and formed the first eleven cricket ground, a beautiful piece of turf, a shade too narrow for its length, bounded on the terrace side by a sharply sloping bank, some fifteen feet deep, and on the other by the precipice leading to the next terrace. At the far end of the ground stood the pavilion, and beside it a little ivy-covered rabbit-hutch for the scorers. Old Wrykynians always claimed that it was the prettiest school ground in England. It certainly had the finest view. From the veranda of the pavilion you could look over three counties.

Wain's house wore an empty and desolate appearance. There were signs of activity, however, inside; and a smell of soap and warm water told of preparations recently completed.

Wyatt took Mike into the matron's room, a small room opening out of the main passage.

"This is Jackson," he said. "Which dormitory is he in, Miss Payne?"

The matron consulted a paper.

"He's in yours, Wyatt."

"Good business. Who's in the other bed? There are going to be three of us, aren't there?"

"Fercira was to have slept there, but we have just heard that he is not coming back this term. He has had to go on a sea voyage for his health."

"Seems queer anyone actually taking the trouble to keep Fereira in the world," said Wyatt. "Come along, Jackson, and I'll show you the room."

They went along the passage, and up a flight of stairs.

"Here you are," said Wyatt.

It was a fair-sized room. The window, heavily barred, looked out over a large garden.

"I used to sleep here alone last term," said Wyatt, "but the house is so full now they've turned it into a domitory."

"I say, I wish these bars weren't here. It would be

rather a rag to get out of the window on to that wall at night, and hop down into the garden and explore," said Mike.

Wyatt looked at him curiously, and moved to the window.

"I'm not going to let you do it, of course," he said, "because you'd go getting caught, and dropped on, which isn't good for one in one's first term; but just to amuse you——"

He jerked at the middle bar, and the next moment he was standing with it in his hand, and the way to the garden was clear.

"By Jove!" said Mike.

"That's simply an object-lesson, you know," said Wyatt, replacing the bar, and pushing the screws back into their putty. "I get out at night myself because I think my health needs it. Besides, it's my last term, anyhow, so it doesn't matter what I do. But if I find you trying to get out in the small hours, there'll be trouble. See?"

"All right," said Mike, reluctantly. "But I wish you'd let me."

"Not if I know it. Promise you won't try it on."

"All right. But, I say, what do you do out there?"

"I shoot at cats with an air-pistol, the beauty of which is that even if you hit them it doesn't hurt—simply keeps them bright and interested in life; and if you miss you've had all the fun anyhow. Have you ever shot at a rocketing cat? Finest mark you can have. Society's latest craze. Buy a pistol and see life."

"I wish you'd let me come."

"I daresay you do. Not a chance, however. Now, if you like, I'll take you over the rest of the school. You'll have to see it sooner or later, so you may as well get it over at once."

CHAPTER IV

AT THE NETS

THERE are few better things in life than a public school summer term. The winter term is good, especially towards the end, and there are points, though not many, about the Easter term: but it is in the summer that one really appreciates public school life. The freedom of it, after the restrictions of even the most easy-going preparatory school, is intoxicating. The change is almost as great as that from public school to 'Varsity.

For Mike the path was made particularly easy. The only drawback to going to a big school for the first time is the fact that one is made to feel so very small and inconspicuous. New boys who have been leading lights at their prep. schools feel it acutely for the first week. At one time it was the custom, if we may believe writers of a generation or so back, for boys to take quite an embarrassing interest in the newcomer. He was asked a rain of questions, and was, generally, in the very centre of the stage. Nowadays an absolute lack of interest is the fashion. A new boy arrives, and there he is, one of a crowd.

Mike was saved this salutary treatment to a large extent, at first by virtue of the greatness of his family, and, later, by his own performances on the cricket field. His three elder brothers were objects of veneration to most Wrykynians, and Mike got a certain amount of reflected glory from them. The brother of first-class cricketers has a dignity of his own. Then Bob was a help. He was on the verge of the cricket team and had been the school full-back for two

...ons. Mike found that people came up and spoke to him, anxious to know if he were Jackson's brother; and became friendly when he replied in the affirmative. Influential relations are a help in every stage of life.

It was Wyatt who gave him his first chance at cricket. There were nets on the first afternoon of term for all old colours of the three teams and a dozen or so of those most likely to fill the vacant places. Wyatt was there, of course. He had got his first eleven cap in the previous season as a mighty hitter and a fair slow bowler. Mike met him crossing the field with his cricket bag.

"Hullo, where are you off to?" asked Wyatt. "Coming to watch the nets?"

Mike had no particular programme for the afternoon. Junior cricket had not begun, and it was a little difficult to know how to fill in the time.

"I tell you what," said Wyatt, "nip into the house and shove on some things, and I'll try and get Burgess to let you have a knock later on."

This suited Mike admirably. A quarter of an hour later he was sitting at the back of the first eleven net, watching the practice.

Burgess, the captain of the Wrykyn team, made no pretence of being a bat. He was the school fast bowler and concentrated his energies on that department of the game. He sometimes took ten minutes at the wicket after everybody else had had an innings, but it was to bowl that he came to the nets.

He was bowling now to one of the old colours whose name Mike did not know. Wyatt and one of the professionals were the other two bowlers. Two nets away Firby-Smith, who had changed his pince-nez for a pair of huge spectacles, was performing rather ineffectively against some very bad bowling. Mike fixed his attention on the first eleven man.

He was evidently a good bat. There was style and power in his batting. He had a way of gliding Burgess's

26

fastest to leg which Mike admired greatly. He was succeeded at the end of a quarter of an hour by another eleven man, and then Bob appeared.

It was soon made evident, that this was not Bob's day. Nobody is at his best on the first day of term; but Bob was worse than he had any right to be. He scratched forward at nearly everything, and when Burgess, who had been resting, took up the ball again, he had each stump uprooted in a regular series in seven balls. Once he skied one of Wyatt's slows over the net behind the wicket; and Mike, jumping up, caught him neatly.

"Thanks," said Bob austerely, as Mike returned the ball to him. He seemed depressed.

Towards the end of the afternoon, Wyatt went up to Burgess.

"Burgess," he said, "see that kid sitting behind the net?"

"With the naked eye," said Burgess. "Why?"

"He's just come to Wain's. He's Bob Jackson's brother, and I've a sort of idea that he's a bit of a bat. I told him I'd ask you if he could have a knock. Why not send him in at the end net? There's nobody there now."

Burgess's amiability off the field equalled his ruthlessness when bowling.

"All right," he said. "Only if you think that I'm going to sweat to bowl to him, you're making a fatal error."

"You needn't do a thing. Just sit and watch. I rather fancy this kid's something special."

Mike put on Wyatt's pads and gloves, borrowed his bat, and walked round into the net.

"Not in a funk, are you?" asked Wyatt, as he passed.

Mike grinned. The fact was that he had far too good an opinion of himself to be nervous. An entirely modest person seldom makes a good batsman. Batting is one of those things which demand first and foremost a thorough belief in oneself. It need not be aggressive, but it must be there.

Wyatt and the professional were the bowlers. Mike had seen enough of Wyatt's bowling to know that it was merely ordinary "slow tosh," and the professional did not look as difficult as Saunders. The first half-dozen balls he played carefully. He was on trial, and he meant to take no risks. Then the professional over-pitched one slightly on the off. Mike jumped out, and got the full face of the bat on to it. The ball hit one of the ropes of the net, and nearly broke it.

"How's that?" said Wyatt, with the smile of an impresario on the first night of a successful play.

"Not bad," admitted Burgess.

A few moments later he was still more complimentary. He got up and took a ball himself.

Mike braced himself up as Burgess began his run. This time he was more than a trifle nervous. The bowling he had had so far had been tame. This would be the real ordeal.

As the ball left Burgess's hand he began instinctively to shape for a forward stroke. Then suddenly he realized that the thing was going to be a yorker, and banged his bat down in the block just as the ball arrived. An unpleasant sensation as of having been struck by a thunderbolt was succeeded by a feeling of relief that he had kept the ball out of his wicket. There are easier things in the world than stopping a fast yorker.

"Well played," said Burgess.

Mike felt like a successful general receiving the thanks of the nation.

The fact that Burgess's next ball knocked middle and off stumps out of the ground saddened him somewhat; but this was the last tragedy that occurred. He could not do much with the bowling beyond stopping it and feeling repetitions of the thunderbolt experience, but he kept up his end; and a short conversation which he had with Burgess at the end of his innings was full of encouragement to one skilled in reading between the lines.

"Thanks awfully," said Mike, referring to the decent manner in which the captain had behaved in letting him bat.

"What school were you at before you came here?" asked Burgess.

"A prep. school in Hampshire," said Mike. "King-Hall's. At a place called Emsworth."

"Get much cricket there?"

"Yes, a good lot. One of the masters, a chap called Westbrook, was an awfully good slow bowler."

Burgess nodded.

"You don't run away, which is something," he said.

Mike turned purple with pleasure at this stately compliment. Then, having waited for further remarks, but gathering from the captain's silence that the audience was at an end, he proceeded to unbuckle his pads. Wyatt overtook him on his way to the house.

"Well played," he said. "I'd no idea you were such hot stuff. You're a regular pro."

"I say," said Mike, gratefully, "it was most awfully decent of you getting Burgess to let me go in."

"Oh, that's all right. If you don't get pushed a bit here you stay for ages in the hundredth game with the cripples and the kids. Now you've shown them what you can do you ought to get into the Under Sixteen team straight away. Probably into the third, too."

"By Jove, that would be all right."

"I asked Burgess afterwards what he thought of your batting, and he said, 'Not bad.' But he says that about everything. It's his highest form of praise. He says it when he wants to let himself go and simply butter up a thing. If you took him to see Trueman bowl, he'd say he wasn't bad. What he meant was that he was jolly struck with your batting, and is going to play you for the Under Sixteen."

"I hope so," said Mike.

The prophecy was fulfilled. On the following Wednesday there was a match between the Under Sixteen and a scratch side. Mike's name was among the Under Sixteen. And on the Saturday he was playing for the third eleven in a trial game.

"This place is ripping," he said to himself, as he saw his name on the list. "Thought I should like it."

And that night he wrote a letter to his father, notifying him of the fact.

CHAPTER V

REVELRY BY NIGHT

A SUCCESSION of events combined to upset Mike during his first fortnight at school. He was far more successful than he had any right to be at his age. There is nothing more heady than success, and if it comes before we are prepared for it, it is apt to throw us off our balance. As a rule, at school, years of wholesome obscurity make us ready for any small triumphs we may achieve at the end of our time there. Mike had skipped these years. He was older than the average new boy, and his batting was undeniable. He knew quite well that he was regarded as a find by the cricket authorities; and the knowledge was not particularly good for him. It did not make him conceited, for his was not a nature at all addicted to conceit. The effect it had on him was to make him excessively pleased with life. And when Mike was pleased with life he always found a difficulty in obeying Authority and its rules. His state of mind was not improved by an interview with Bob.

Some evil genius put it into Bob's mind that it was his duty to be, if only for one performance, the Heavy Elder Brother to Mike; to give him good advice. It is never the smallest use for an elder brother to attempt to do anything for the good of a younger brother at school, for the latter rebels automatically against such interference in his concerns; but Bob did not know this. He only knew that he had received a letter from home, in which his mother had assumed without evidence that he was leading Mike by the hand round the pitfalls of life at Wrykyn; and his conscience smote him. Beyond asking him occasionally, when they met, how he was getting on (a question to which Mike invariably replied, "Oh, all right"), he was not aware of having done anything brotherly towards the youngster. So he asked Mike to tea in his study one afternoon before going to the nets.

Mike arrived, sidling into the study in the half-sheepish, half-defiant manner peculiar to small brothers in the presence of their elders, and stared in silence at the photographs on the walls. Bob was changing into his cricket things. The atmosphere was one of constraint and awkwardness.

The arrival of tea was the cue for conversation.

"Well, how are you getting on?" asked Bob.

"Oh, all right," said Mike.

Silence.

"Sugar?" asked Bob.

"Thanks," said Mike.

"How many lumps?"

"Two, please."

"Cake?"

"Thanks."

Silence.

Bob pulled himself together.

"Like Wain's?"

"Ripping."

"I asked Firby-Smith to keep an eye on you," said Bob.

"What!" said Mike.

The mere idea of a worm like the Gazeka being told to keep an eye on *him* was degrading.

"He said he'd look after you," added Bob, making things worse.

Look after him! Him! M. Jackson, of the third eleven!!!

Mike helped himself to another chunk of cake, and spoke crushingly.

"He needn't trouble," he said. "I can look after myself all right, thanks."

Bob saw an opening for the entry of the Heavy Elder Brother.

"Look here, Mike," he said, "I'm only saying it for your good——"

I should like to state here that it was not Bob's habit to go about the world telling people things solely for their good. He was only doing it now to ease his conscience.

"Yes?" said Mike coldly.

"It's only this. You know, I should keep an eye on myself if I were you. There's nothing that gets a chap so barred here as side."

"What do you mean?" said Mike, outraged.

"Oh, I'm not saying anything against you so far," said Bob. "You've been all right up to now. What I mean to say is, you've got on so well at cricket, in the third and so on, there's just a chance you might start throwing your weight around soon, if you don't watch yourself. I'm not saying a word against you so far, of course. Only you see what I mean."

Mike's feelings were too deep for words. In sombre silence he reached out for the jam; while Bob, satisfied that he had delivered his message in a pleasant and tactful manner, filled his cup, and cast about him for further words of wisdom.

"Seen you about with Wyatt a good deal," he said at length.

"Yes," said Mike.

"Like him?"

"Yes," said Mike cautiously.

"You know," said Bob, "I shouldn't—I mean, I should take care what you're doing with Wyatt."

"What do you mean?"

"Well, he's an awfully good chap, of course, but still——"

"Still what?"

"Well, I mean, he's the sort of chap who'll probably get into some thundering row before he leaves. He doesn't care a hang what he does. He's that sort of chap. He's never been dropped on yet, but if you go on breaking rules you're bound to be sooner or later. Thing is, it doesn't matter much for him, because he's leaving at the end of the term. But don't let him drag you into anything. Not that he would try to. But you might think it was the done thing to imitate him, and the first thing you knew you'd be dropped on by Wain or somebody. See what I mean?"

Bob was well-intentioned, but tact did not enter greatly into his composition.

"What rot!" said Mike.

"All right. But don't you go doing it. I'm going over to the nets. I see Burgess has shoved you down for them. You'd better be going and changing. Stick on here a bit, though, if you want any more tea. I've got to be off myself."

Mike changed for net-practice in a ferment of spiritual injury. It was maddening to be treated as an infant who had to be looked after. He felt very sore against Bob.

A good innings at the third eleven net, followed by some strenuous fielding in the deep, soothed his ruffled feelings to a large extent; and all might have been well but for the intervention of Firby-Smith.

That youth, all spectacles and front teeth, met Mike at the door of Wain's.

"Ah, I wanted to see you, young man," he said. (Mike disliked being called "young man.") "Come up to my study."

Mike followed him in silence to his study, and preserved his silence till Firby-Smith, having deposited his cricket-bag in a corner of the room and examined himself carefully in a looking-glass that hung over the mantelpiece, spoke again.

"I've been hearing all about you, young man." Mike shuffled.

34

"You're a frightful character from all accounts." Mike could not think of anything to say that was not rude, so said nothing.

"Your brother has asked me to keep an eye on you."

Mike's soul began to tie itself into knots again. He was just at the age when one is most sensitive to patronage and most resentful of it.

"I promised I would," said the Gazeka, turning round and examining himself in the mirror again. "You'll get on all right if you behave yourself. Don't make a frightful row in the house. Don't cheek your elders and betters. Wash. That's all. Buzz off."

Mike had a vague idea of sacrificing his career to the momentary pleasure of flinging a chair at the head of the house. Overcoming this feeling, he walked out of the room, and up to his dormitory to change.

In the dormitory that night the feeling of revolt, of wanting to do something actively illegal, increased. Like "Eric," he burned, not with shame and remorse, but with rage and all that sort of thing. He dropped off to sleep full of half-formed plans for asserting himself. He was awakened from a dream in which he was batting against Firby-Smith's bowling, and hitting it into space every time, by a slight sound. He opened his eyes, and saw a dark figure silhouetted against the light of the window. He sat up in bed.

"Hullo," he said. "Is that you, Wyatt?"

"Are you awake?" said Wyatt. "Sorry if I've spoiled your beauty sleep."

"Are you going out?"

"I am," said Wyatt. "The cats are particularly strong on the wind just now. Mustn't miss a chance like this. Specially as there's a good moon, too. I shall be deadly."

"I say, can't I come too?"

A moonlight prowl, with or without an air-pistol, would just have suited Mike's mood.

"No, you can't," said Wyatt. "When I'm caught, as I'm morally certain to be some day, or night rather, they're bound to ask if you've ever been out as well as me. Then you'll be able to put your hand on your little heart and do a big George Washington act. You'll find that useful when the time comes."

"Do you think you will be caught?"

"Shouldn't be surprised. Anyhow, you stay where you are. Go to sleep and dream that you're playing for the school against Ripton. So long."

And Wyatt, laying the bar he had extracted on the window-sill, wriggled out. Mike saw him disappearing along the wall.

It was all very well for Wyatt to tell him to go to sleep, but it was not so easy to do it. The room was almost light; and Mike always found it difficult to sleep unless it was dark. He turned over on his side and shut his eyes, but he had never felt wider awake. Twice he heard the quarters chime from the school clock; and the second time he gave up the struggle. He got out of bed and went to the window. It was a lovely night, just the sort of night on which, if he had been at home, he would have been out after moths with a torch.

A sharp yowl from an unseen cat told of Wyatt's presence somewhere in the big garden. He would have given much to be with him, but he realized that he was on parole. He had promised not to leave the house, and there was an end of it.

He turned away from the window and sat down on his bed. Then a beautiful, consoling thought came to him. He had given his word that he would not go into the garden, but nothing had been said about exploring inside the house. It was quite late now. Everybody would be in bed. It would be quite safe. And there must be all sorts of things to interest the visitor in Wain's part of the house. Food, perhaps. Mike felt that he could just do

36

with a biscuit. And there were bound to be biscuits on the sideboard in Wain's dining-room.

He crept quietly out of the dormitory.

He had been long enough in the house to know the way, in spite of the fact that all was darkness. Down the stairs, along the passage to the left, and up a few more stairs at the end. The beauty of the position was that the dining-room had two doors, one leading into Wain's part of the house, the other into the boys' section. Any interruption that there might be would come from the further door.

To make himself more secure he locked that door; then, turning on the light, he proceeded to look about him.

Mr. Wain's dining-room repaid inspection. There were the remains of supper on the table. Mike cut himself some cheese and took some biscuits from the box, feeling that he was doing himself well. This was life. There was a little soda-water in the syphon. He finished it. As it swished into the glass, it made a noise that seemed to him like three hundred Niagaras; but nobody else in the house appeared to have noticed it.

He took some more biscuits, and an apple.

After which, feeling a new man, he examined the room.

And this was where the trouble began.

On a table in one corner stood a small gramophone. And gramophones happened to be Mike's particular craze.

All thought of risk left him. The soda-water may have got into his head, or he may have been in a particularly reckless mood, as indeed he was. The fact remains that he put on the first record that came to hand and switched on.

The next moment, a very loud voice announced that Mr. Godfrey Field would sing "The Quaint Old Bird." And, after a few preliminary chords, Mr. Field actually did so.

"*Auntie went to Aldershot in a Paris pom-pom hat.*"

Mike stood and drained it in.

". . . *Good gracious* [sang Mr. Field], *what was that?*"

It was a rattling at the handle of the door. A rattling that turned almost immediately into a spirited banging.

A voice accompanied the banging. "Who is there?" inquired the voice. Mike recognized it as Mr. Wain's. He was not alarmed. The man who holds the ace of trumps has no need to be alarmed. His position was impregnable. The enemy was held in check by the locked door, while the other door offered an admirable and instantaneous way of escape.

Mike crept across the room on tiptoe and opened the window. It had occurred to him, just in time, that if Mr. Wain, on entering the room, found that the occupant had retired by way of the boys' part of the house, he might possibly obtain a clue to his identity. If, on the other hand, he opened the window, suspicion would be diverted. Mike had not read his "Raffles" for nothing.

The hand-rattling was resumed. This was good. So long as the frontal attack was kept up, there was no chance of his being taken in the rear—his only danger.

He stopped the gramophone, which had been pegging away patiently at "The Quaint Old Bird" all the time, and reflected. It seemed a pity to evacuate the position and ring down the curtain on what was, to date, the most exciting episode of his life; but he must not overdo the thing, and get caught. At any moment the noise might bring reinforcements to the besieging force, though it was not likely, for the dining-room was a long way from the dormitories; and it might flash upon their minds that there were two entrances to the room. Or the same bright thought might come to Wain himself.

"Now what," pondered Mike, "would A. J. Raffles have done in a case like this? Suppose he'd been after somebody's jewels, and found that they were after him, and he'd locked one door, and could get away by the other."

The answer was simple.

"He'd clear out," thought Mike.

Two minutes later he was in bed.

He lay there, tingling all over with the consciousness of having played a masterly game, when suddenly a gruesome idea came to him, and he sat up, breathless. Suppose Wain took it into his head to make a tour of the dormitories, to see that all was well! Wyatt was still in the garden somewhere, blissfully unconscious of what was going on indoors. He would be caught for a certainty!

CHAPTER VI

IN WHICH A TIGHT CORNER IS EVADED

FOR a moment the situation paralysed Mike. Then he began to be equal to it. In times of excitement one thinks rapidly and clearly. The main point, the kernel of the whole thing, was that he must get into the garden somehow, and warn Wyatt. And at the same time, he must keep Mr. Wain from coming to the dormitory. He jumped out of bed, and dashed down the dark stairs.

He had taken care to close the dining-room door after him. It was open now, and he could hear somebody moving inside the room. Evidently his retreat had been made just in time.

He knocked at the door, and went in.

Mr. Wain was standing at the window, looking out. He spun round at the knock, and stared in astonishment at Mike's pyjama-clad figure. Mike, in spite of his anxiety, could barely check a laugh. Mr. Wain was a tall, thin man, with a serious face partially obscured by a grizzled beard. He wore spectacles, through which he peered owlishly at Mike. His body was wrapped in a brown dressing-gown. His hair was ruffled. He looked like some weird bird.

"Please, sir, I thought I heard a noise," said Mike.

Mr. Wain continued to stare.

"What are you doing here?" said he at last.

"Thought I heard a noise, please, sir."

"A noise?"

"Please, sir, a row."

"You thought you heard——"

The thing seemed to be worrying Mr. Wain.

"So I came down, sir," said Mike.

The house-master's giant brain still appeared to be somewhat clouded. He looked about him, and, catching sight of the gramophone, drew inspiration from it.

"Did *you* turn on the gramophone?" he asked.

"*Me*, sir!" said Mike, with the air of a bishop accused of contributing to the *Police News*.

"Of course not, of course not," said Mr. Wain hurriedly. "Of course not. I don't know why I asked. All this is very unsettling. What are you doing here?"

"Thought I heard a noise, please, sir."

"A noise?"

"A row, sir."

If it was Mr. Wain's wish that he should spend the night playing Massa Tambo to his Massa Bones, it was not for him to balk the house-master's innocent pleasure. He was prepared to continue the snappy dialogue till breakfast-time.

"I think there must have been a burglar in here, Jackson."

"Looks like it, sir."

"I found the window open."

"He's probably in the garden, sir."

Mr. Wain looked out into the garden with an annoyed expression, as if its behaviour in letting burglars be in it struck him as unworthy of a respectable garden.

"He might be still in the house," said Mr. Wain, ruminatively.

"Not likely, sir."

"You think not?"

"Wouldn't be such a fool, sir. I mean, such an ass, sir."

"Perhaps you are right, Jackson."

"I shouldn't wonder if he was hiding in the shrubbery, sir."

Mr. Wain looked at the shrubbery, as who should say, "*Et tu, Brute!*"

"By Jove! I think I see him," cried Mike.

41

He ran to the window, and vaulted through it on to the lawn. An inarticulate protest from Mr. Wain, rendered speechless by this move just as he had been beginning to recover his faculties, and he was running across the lawn into the shrubbery. He felt that all was well. There might be a bit of a row on his return, but he could always plead overwhelming excitement.

Wyatt was round at the back somewhere, and the problem was how to get back without being seen from the dining-room window. Fortunately a belt of evergreens ran along the path right up to the house. Mike worked his way cautiously through these till he was out of sight, then tore for the regions at the back.

The moon had gone behind the clouds, and it was not easy to find a way through the bushes. Twice branches sprang out from nowhere, and hit Mike smartly over the shins, eliciting sharp howls of pain.

On the second of these occasions a low voice spoke from somewhere on his right.

"Who on earth's that?" it said.

Mike stopped.

"Is that you, Wyatt? I say——"

"Jackson!"

The moon came out again, and Mike saw Wyatt clearly. His knees were covered with mould. He had evidently been crouching in the bushes on all fours.

"You young ass," said Wyatt. "You promised me that you wouldn't get out."

"Yes, I know, but——"

"I heard you crashing through the shrubbery like a hundred elephants. If you *must* get out at night and chance being sacked, you might at least have the sense to walk quietly."

"Yes, but you don't understand."

And Mike rapidly explained the situation.

"But how the dickens did he hear you, if you were in the dining-room?" asked Wyatt. "It's miles from his bedroom. You must tread like a policeman."

"It wasn't that. The thing was, you see, it was rather a rotten thing to do, I suppose, but I turned on the gramophone."

"You—*what*?"

"The gramophone. It started playing 'The Quaint Old Bird.' Ripping it was, till Wain came along."

Wyatt doubled up with noiseless laughter.

"You're a genius," he said. "I never saw such a man. Well, what's the game now? What's the idea?"

"I think you'd better nip back along the wall and in through the window, and I'll go back to the dining-room. Then it'll be all right if Wain comes and looks into the dorm. Or, if you like, you might come down too, as if you'd just woke up and thought you'd heard a row."

"That's not a bad idea. All right. You dash along then. I'll get back."

Mr. Wain was still in the dining-room, drinking in the beauties of the summer night through the open window. He gibbered slightly when Mike reappeared.

"Jackson! What do you mean by running about outside the house in this way! I shall punish you very heavily. I shall certainly report the matter to the headmaster. I will not have boys rushing about the garden in their pyjamas. You will catch an exceedingly bad cold. You will do me two hundred lines, Latin and English. Exceedingly so. I will not have it. Did you not hear me call to you?"

"Please, sir, so excited," said Mike, standing outside with his hands on the sill.

"You have no business to be excited. I will not have it. It is exceedingly impertinent of you."

"Please, sir, may I come in?"

"Come in! Of course, come in. Have you no sense boy? You are laying the seeds of a bad cold. Come in at once."

Mike clambered through the window.

"I couldn't find him, sir. He must have got out of the garden."

"Undoubtedly," said Mr. Wain. "Undoubtedly so. It was very wrong of you to search for him. You might have been seriously injured. Exceedingly so."

He was about to say more on the subject when Wyatt strolled into the room. Wyatt wore the rather dazed expression of one who has been aroused from deep sleep. He yawned before he spoke.

"I thought I heard a noise, sir," he said.

He called Mr. Wain "father" in private, "sir" in public. The presence of Mike made this a public occasion.

"Has there been a burglary?"

"Yes," said Mike, "only he has got away."

"Shall I go out into the garden, and have a look round, sir?" asked Wyatt helpfully.

The question stung Mr. Wain into active eruption once more.

"Under no circumstances whatever," he said excitedly. "Stay where you are, James. I will not have boys running about my garden at night. It is preposterous. Inordinately so. Both of you go to bed immediately. I shall not speak to you again on this subject. I must be obeyed instantly. You hear me, Jackson? James, you understand me? To bed at once. And, if I find you outside your dormitory again tonight, you will both be punished with extreme severity. I will not have this lax and reckless behaviour."

"But the burglar, sir?" said Wyatt.

"We might catch him, sir," said Mike.

Mr. Wain's manner changed to a slow and stately sarcasm, in much the same way as a motor-car changes gear.

"I was under the impression," he said, in the heavy way almost invariably affected by weak masters in their dealings with the obstreperous, "I was distinctly under the impression that I had ordered you to retire immediately to your dormitory. It is possible that you mistook my meaning. In that case I shall be happy to repeat what I said. It is

44

also in my mind that I threatened to punish you with the utmost severity if you did not retire at once. In these circumstances, James—and you, Jackson—you will doubtless see the necessity of complying with my wishes."

They made it so.

CHAPTER VII

IN WHICH MIKE IS DISCUSSED

TREVOR and Clowes, of Donaldson's, were sitting in their study a week after the gramophone incident, preparatory to going on the river. At least Trevor was in the study, getting tea ready. Clowes was on the window-sill, one leg in the room, the other outside, hanging over space. He loved to sit in this attitude, watching someone else work, and giving his views on life to whoever would listen to them. Clowes was tall, and looked sad, which he was not. Trevor was shorter, and very much in earnest over all that he did. On the present occasion he was measuring out tea with a concentration worthy of a general planning a campaign.

"One for the pot," said Clowes.

"All right," breathed Trevor. "Come and help, you slacker."

"Too busy."

"You aren't doing a stroke."

"My lad, I'm thinking of Life. That's a thing you couldn't do. I often say to people, 'Good chap, Trevor, but can't think of Life. Give him a teapot and half a pound of butter to mess about with,' I say, 'and he's all right. But when it comes to deep thought, where is he? Among the also-rans.' That's what I say."

"Silly ass," said Trevor, slicing bread. "What particular rot were you thinking about just then? What fun it was sitting back and watching other fellows work, I should think."

46

"My mind at the moment," said Clowes, "was tensely occupied with the problem of brothers at school. Have you got any brothers, Trevor?"

"One. Couple of years younger than me. I say, we shall want some more jam tomorrow. Better order it today."

"See it done, Tigellinus, as our old pal Nero used to remark. Where is he? Your brother, I mean."

"Marlborough."

"That shows your sense. I have always had a high opinion of your sense, Trevor. If you'd been a silly ass, you'd have let your people send him here."

"Why not? Shouldn't have minded."

"I withdraw what I said about your sense. Consider it unsaid. I have a brother myself. Aged fifteen. Not a bad chap in his way. Like the heroes of the school stories. 'Big blue eyes literally bubbling over with fun.' At least, I suppose it's fun to him. Cheek's what I call it. My people wanted to send him here. I lodged a protest. I said, 'One Clowes is ample for any public school.'"

"You were right there," said Trevor.

"I said, 'One Clowes is luxury, two excess.' I pointed out that I was just on the verge of becoming rather a blood at Wrykyn, and that I didn't want the work of years spoiled by a brother who would think it a rag to tell fellows who respected and admired me——"

"Such as who?"

"——Anecdotes of a chequered infancy. There are stories about me which only my brother knows. Did I want them spread about the school? No, laddie, I did not. Hence, we see my brother two terms ago, packing up his little box, and tooling off to Rugby. And here am I at Wrykyn, with an unstained reputation, loved by all who know me, revered by all who don't; courted by boys, fawned upon by masters. People's faces brighten when I throw them a nod. If I frown——"

"Oh, come on," said Trevor.

Bread and jam and cake monopolized Clowes's attention

for the next quarter of an hour. At the end of that period, however, he returned to his subject.

"After the serious business of the meal was concluded, and a simple hymn had been sung by those present," he said, "Mr. Clowes resumed his very interesting remarks. We were on the subject of brothers at school. Now, take the melancholy case of Jackson Brothers. My heart bleeds for Bob."

"Jackson's all right. What's wrong with him? Besides, naturally, young Jackson came to Wrykyn when all his brothers had been here."

"What a rotten argument. It's just the one used by chaps' people, too. They think how nice it will be for all the sons to have been at the same school. It may be all right after they've left, but while they're there, it's the limit. You say Jackson's all right. At present, perhaps, he is. But the term's hardly started yet."

"Well?"

"Look here, what's at the bottom of this sending young brothers to the same school as elder brothers?"

"Elder brother can keep an eye on him, I suppose."

"That's just it. For once in your life you've touched the spot. In other words, Bob Jackson is practically responsible for the kid. That's where the whole rotten trouble starts."

"Why?"

"Well, what happens? He either lets the kid rip, in which case he may find himself any morning in the pleasant position of having to explain to his people exactly why it is that little Willie has just received the boot, and why he didn't look after him better: or he spends all his spare time shadowing him to see that he doesn't get into trouble. He feels that his reputation hangs on the kid's conduct, so he broods over him like a policeman, which is pretty rotten for him and maddens the kid, who looks on him as no sportsman. Bob seems to be trying the first way, which is what I should do myself. It's all right, so far, but, as I said, the term's only just started."

"Young Jackson seems all right. What's wrong with him? He doesn't stick on side anyway, which he might easily do, considering his cricket."

"There's nothing wrong with him in that way. I've talked to him several times at the nets, and he's very decent. But his getting into trouble hasn't anything to do with us. It's the masters you've got to consider."

"What's up? Does he rag?"

"From what I gather from fellows in his form he's got a genius for ragging. Thinks of things that don't occur to anybody else, and does them, too."

"He never seems to be in extra. One always sees him about on half-holidays."

"That's always the way with that sort of chap. He keeps on wriggling out of small rows till he thinks he can do anything he likes without being dropped on, and then all of a sudden he finds himself up to the eyebrows in a record smash. I don't say young Jackson will land himself like that. All I say is that he's just the sort who does. He's asking for trouble. Besides, who do you see him about with all the time?"

"He's generally with Wyatt when I meet him."

"Yes. Well, then!"

"What's wrong with Wyatt? He's one of the decentest chaps in the school."

"I know. But he's working up for a tremendous row one of these days, unless he leaves before it comes off. The odds are, if Jackson's so thick with him, that he'll be roped into it too. Wyatt wouldn't land him if he could help it, but he probably wouldn't realize what he was letting the kid in for. For instance, I happen to know that Wyatt breaks out of his dorm every other night. I don't know if he takes Jackson with him. I shouldn't think so. But there's nothing to prevent Jackson following him on his own. And if you're caught at that game, it's the boot every time."

Trevor looked disturbed.

"Somebody ought to speak to Bob."

"What's the good? Why worry him? Bob couldn't do anything. You'd only make him do the policeman business, which he hasn't time for, and which is bound to make rows between them. Better leave him alone."

"I don't know. It would be a beastly thing for Bob if the kid did get into a really bad row."

"If you must tell anybody, tell the Gazeka. He's head of Wain's, and has got far more chance of keeping an eye on Jackson than Bob has."

"The Gazeka is a fool."

"All front teeth and side. Still, he's on the spot. But what's the good of worrying. It's nothing to do with us, anyhow. Let's stagger out, shall we?"

Trevor's conscientious nature, however, made it impossible for him to drop the matter. It disturbed him all the time that he and Clowes were on the river; and, walking back to the house, he resolved to see Bob about it during preparation.

He found him in his study, oiling a bat.

"I say, Bob," he said, "look here. Are you busy?"

"No. Why?"

"It's this way. Clowes and I were talking——"

"If Clowes was there he was probably talking. Well?"

"About your brother."

"Oh, by Jove," said Bob, sitting up. "That reminds me. I forgot to get the evening paper. Did he get his century all right?"

"Who?" asked Trevor, bewildered.

"My brother, J.W. He'd made sixty-three not out against Kent in this morning's paper. What happened?"

"I didn't get a paper either. I didn't mean that brother. I meant the one here."

"Oh, Mike? What's Mike been up to?"

"Nothing as yet, that I know of; but, I say, you know, he seems a great pal of Wyatt's."

"I know. I spoke to him about it."

"Oh, you did? That's all right, then."

"Not that there's anything wrong with Wyatt."

"Not a bit. Only he is rather mucking about this term, I hear. It's his last, so I suppose he wants to have a rag."

"Don't blame him."

"Nor do I. Rather rot, though, if he lugged your brother into a row by accident."

"I should get blamed. I think I'll speak to him again."

"I should, I think."

"I hope he isn't idiot enough to go out at night with Wyatt. If Wyatt likes to risk it, all right. That's his look out. But it won't do for Mike to go playing the goat too."

"Clowes suggested putting Firby-Smith on to him. He'd have more chance, being in the same house, of seeing that he didn't come a mucker than you would."

"I've done that. Smith said he'd speak to him."

"That's all right then. Is that a new bat?"

"Got it today. Smashed my other yesterday—against the School House."

Donaldson's had played a friendly with the School House during the last two days, and had beaten them.

"I thought I heard it go. You were rather in form."

"Better than at the beginning of the term, anyhow. I simply couldn't do a thing then. But my last three innings have been 33 not out, 18, and 51."

"I should think you're bound to get your first all right."

"Hope so. I see Mike's playing for the second against the O.W.s."

"Yes. Pretty good for his first term. You have a pro to coach you in the holidays, don't you?"

"Yes. I didn't go to him much this last time. I was away a lot. But Mike fairly lived inside the net."

"Well, it's not been chucked away. I suppose he'll get his first next year. There'll be a big clearing-out of colours at the end of this term. Nearly all the first are leaving. Henfrey'll be captain, I expect."

"Saunders, the pro at home, always says that Mike's

going to be the star cricketer of the family. Better than J.W. even, he thinks. I asked him what he thought of me, and he said, 'You'll be making a lot of runs some day, Mr. Bob.' There's a subtle difference, isn't there? I shall have Mike cutting me out before I leave school if I'm not careful."

"Sort of infant prodigy," said Trevor. "Don't think he's quite up to it yet, though."

He went back to his study, and Bob, having finished his oiling and washed his hands, started on his Thucydides. And, in the stress of wrestling with the speech of an apparently delirious Athenian general, whose remarks seemed to contain nothing even remotely resembling sense and coherence, he allowed the question of Mike's welfare to fade from his mind like a dissolving view.

CHAPTER VIII

A ROW WITH THE TOWN

THE beginning of a big row, one of those rows which turn a school upside down like a volcanic eruption and provide old boys with something to talk about, when they meet, for years, is not unlike the beginning of a thunderstorm.

You are walking along one seemingly fine day, when suddenly there is a hush, and there falls on you from space one big drop. The next moment the thing has begun, and you are standing in a shower-bath. It is just the same with a row. Some trivial episode occurs, and in an instant the place is in a ferment. It was so with the great picnic at Wrykyn.

The bare outlines of the beginning of this affair are included in a letter which Mike wrote to his father on the Sunday following the Old Wrykynian matches.

This was the letter:

"DEAR FATHER,

"Thanks awfully for your letter. I hope you are quite well. I have been getting on all right at cricket lately. My scores since I wrote last have been o in a scratch game (the sun got in my eyes just as I played, and I got bowled); 15 for the third against an eleven of masters (without G. B. Jones, the Surrey man, and Spence); 28 not out in the Under Sixteen game; and 30 in a form match. Rather decent. Yesterday one of the men put down for the second against the O.W.s second couldn't play because his father was very ill, so I played. Wasn't it luck? It's the first time I've played for the second. I didn't do much, because I didn't get an innings. They stop the cricket on O.W. matches day because they have a lot of rotten Greek plays and things which take up a frightful time, and half the chaps are acting, so we stop from lunch to four. Rot I call it. So I didn't go in, because they won the toss and made 215, and by the time we'd made 140 for 6 it was close of play. They'd stuck me in eighth wicket. Rather rot. Still, I may get another shot. And I made rather a decent catch at mid-on. Low down. I had to dive for it. Bob played for the first, but didn't do much. He was run out after he'd got ten. I believe he's rather sick about it.

"Rather a rummy thing happened after lock-up. I wasn't in it, but a fellow called Wyatt (awfully decent chap. He's Wain's step-son, only they dislike one another) told me about it. He was in it all right. There's a dinner after the matches on O.W. day, and some of the chaps were going back to their houses after it when they got into a row with a lot of spivs and there was rather a row. There was a policeman mixed up in it somehow, only I don't quite know where he comes in. I'll find out and tell you next time I write. Love to everybody. Tell Marjory I'll write to her in a day or two.

"Your loving son,
"MIKE."

"P.S.—I say, I suppose you couldn't send me five bob, could you? I'm rather broke.

"P.P.S.—Half-a-crown would do, only I'd rather it was five bob."

And, on the back of the envelope, these words: "Or a bob would be better than nothing."

The outline of the case was as Mike had stated. But there were certain details of some importance which had not come to his notice when he sent the letter. On the Monday they were public property.

The thing had happened after this fashion. At the conclusion of the day's cricket, all those who had been playing in the four elevens which the school put into the field against the old boys, together with the school choir, were entertained by the headmaster to supper in the Great Hall. The banquet, lengthened by speeches, songs, and recitations which the reciters imagined to be songs, lasted, as a rule, till about ten o'clock, when the revellers were supposed to go back to their houses by the nearest route, and turn in. This was the official programme. The school usually performed it with certain modifications and improvements.

About midway between Wrykyn, the school, and Wrykyn, the town, there stands on an island in the centre of the road a solitary lamp-post. It was the custom, and had been the custom for generations back, for the diners to trudge off to this lamp-post, dance round it for some minutes singing the school song or whatever happened to be the popular song of the moment, and then race back to their houses. Antiquity had given the custom a sort of sanctity, and the authorities, if they knew—which they must have done—never interfered.

But there were others.

Wrykyn, the town, was peculiarly rich in "gangs of youths." Like the vast majority of the inhabitants of the place, they seemed to have no work of any kind whatsoever to occupy their time, which they used, accordingly, to spend prowling about and indulging in a mild, brainless, rural type of hooliganism. They seldom proceeded to practical rowdyism except with the school. As a rule, they amused themselves by shouting rude chaff. The school regarded them with a lofty contempt, much as an Oxford man regards the townee. The school was always anxious for a row, but it was the unwritten law that only in special circumstances should they proceed to active measures. A curious dislike for school-and-town rows and most misplaced severity in dealing with the offenders when they took place, were among the few flaws in the otherwise admirable character of the headmaster of Wrykyn. It was understood that one scragged town types at one's own risk, and, as a rule, it was not considered worth it.

But after an excellent supper and much singing and joviality, one's views are apt to alter. Risks which before supper seemed great, show a tendency to dwindle.

When, therefore, the twenty or so Wrykynians who were dancing round the lamp-post were aware, in the midst of their festivities, that they were being observed and criticized by an equal number of townees, and that the criticisms were, as usual, essentially candid and personal, they found themselves forgetting the headmaster's prejudices and feeling only that these outsiders must be put to the sword as speedily as possible, for the honour of the school.

Possibly, if the town brigade had stuck to a purely verbal form of attack, all might yet have been peace. Words can be overlooked.

But tomatoes cannot.

No man of spirit can bear to be pelted with over-ripe tomatoes for any length of time without feeling that if the thing goes on much longer he will be reluctantly compelled to take steps.

In the present crisis, the first tomato was enough to set matters moving.

As the two armies stood facing each other in silence under the dim and mysterious rays of the lamp, it suddenly whizzed out from the enemy's ranks, and hit Wyatt on the right ear.

There was a moment of suspense. Wyatt took out his handkerchief and wiped his face, over which the succulent vegetable had spread itself.

"I don't know how you fellows are going to pass the evening," he said quietly. "My idea of a good after-dinner game is to try and find the chap who threw that. Anybody coming?"

For the first five minutes it was as even a fight as one could have wished to see. It raged up and down the road without a pause, now in a solid mass, now splitting up into little groups. The science was on the side of the school.

Most Wrykynians knew how to box to a certain extent. But, at any rate at first, it was no time for science. To be scientific one must have an opponent who observes at least the more important rules of the ring. It is impossible to do the latest ducks and hooks taught you by the instructor if your antagonist butts you in the chest, and then kicks your shins, while some dear friend of his, of whose presence you had no idea, hits you at the same time on the back of the head. The greatest expert would lose his science in such circumstances.

Probably what gave the school the victory in the end was the righteousness of their cause. They were smarting under a sense of injury, and there is nothing that adds a force to one's blows and a recklessness to one's style of delivering them more than a sense of injury.

Wyatt, one side of his face still showing traces of the tomato, led the school with a vigour that could not be resisted. He very seldom lost his temper, but he did draw the line at bad tomatoes.

Presently the school noticed that the enemy were vanishing little by little into the darkness which concealed the town. Barely a dozen remained. And their lonely condition seemed to be borne in upon these by a simultaneous brain-wave, for they suddenly gave the fight up, and stampeded as one man.

The leaders were beyond recall, but two remained, tackled low by Wyatt and Clowes after the fashion of the football field.

The school gathered round its prisoners, panting. The scene of the conflict had shifted little by little to a spot some fifty yards from where it had started. By the side of the road at this point was a green, depressed-looking pond. Gloomy in the daytime, it looked unspeakable at night. It struck Wyatt, whose finer feelings had been entirely blotted out by tomato, as an ideal place in which to bestow the captives.

"Let's chuck 'em in there," he said.

The idea was welcomed gladly by all, except the prisoners. A move was made towards the pond, and the procession had halted on the brink, when a new voice made itself heard.

"Now then," it said, "what's all this?"

A stout figure in policeman's uniform was standing surveying them with the aid of a flashlight.

"What's all this?"

"It's all right," said Wyatt.

"All right, is it? What's on?"

One of the prisoners spoke.

"Make 'em leave hold of us, Mr. Butt. They're a-going to chuck us in the pond."

"Ho!" said the policeman, with a change in his voice. "Ho, are they? Come now, young gentleman, a lark's a lark, but you ought to know where to stop."

"It's anything but a lark," said Wyatt in the creamy voice he used when feeling particularly savage. "We're the Strong Right Arm of Justice. That's what we are. This isn't a lark, it's an execution."

"I don't want none of your lip, whoever you are," said Mr. Butt, understanding but dimly, and suspecting impudence by instinct.

"This is quite a private matter," said Wyatt. "You run along on your beat. You can't do anything here."

"Ho!"

"Shove 'em in, you chaps."

"Stop!" From Mr. Butt.

"Oo-er!" From prisoner number one.

There was a sounding splash as willing hands urged the first of the captives into the depths. He ploughed his way to the bank, scrambled out, and vanished.

Wyatt turned to the other prisoner.

"You'll have the worst of it, going in second. He'll have churned up the mud a bit. Don't swallow more than you can help, or you'll go getting typhoid. I expect there are leeches and things there, but if you nip out quick they may not get on to you. Carry on, you chaps."

It was here that the regrettable incident occurred. Just

as the second prisoner was being launched, Constable Butt, determined to assert himself even at the eleventh hour, sprang forward, and seized the captive by the arm. A drowning man will clutch at a straw. A man about to be hurled into an excessively dirty pond will clutch at a stout policeman. The prisoner did.

Constable Butt represented his one link with dry land. As he came within reach he attached himself to his tunic with the vigour and concentration of a limpet.

At the same moment the executioners gave their man the final heave. The policeman realized his peril too late. A medley of noises made the peaceful night hideous. A howl from the townee, a yell from the policeman, a cheer from the launching party, a frightened squawk from some birds in a neighbouring tree, and a splash compared with which the first had been as nothing, and all was over.

The dark waters were lashed into a maelstrom; and then two streaming figures squelched up the further bank.

The school stood in silent consternation. It was no occasion for light apologies.

"Do you know," said Wyatt, as he watched the Law shaking the water from itself on the other side of the pond, "I'm not half sure that we hadn't better be moving!"

CHAPTER IX

BEFORE THE STORM

YOUR real, devastating row has many points of resemblance with a prairie fire. A man on a prairie lights his pipe, and throws away the match. The flame catches a bunch of dry grass, and, before anyone can realize what is happening, sheets of fire are racing over the country; and the interested neighbours are following their example. (I have already compared a row with a thunderstorm; but both comparisons may stand. In dealing with so vast a matter as a row there must be no stint.)

The tomato which hit Wyatt in the face was the thrown-away match. But for the unerring aim of the town marksman great events would never have happened. A tomato is a trivial thing (though it is possible that the man whom it hits may not think so), but in the present case, it was the direct cause of epoch-making trouble.

The tomato hit Wyatt. Wyatt, with others, went to look for the thrower. The remnants of the thrower's friends were placed in the pond, and "with them," as they say in the courts of law, Police Constable Alfred Butt.

Following the chain of events, we find Mr. Butt, having prudently changed his clothes, calling upon the headmaster.

The headmaster was grave and sympathetic; Mr. Butt fierce and revengeful.

The imagination of the Force is proverbial. Nurtured on motor-cars and fed with stop-watches, it has become world-famous. Mr. Butt gave free rein to it.

"Threw me in, they did, sir. Yes, sir."

"Threw you in!"

"Yes, sir. *Plop!*" said Mr. Butt, with a certain sad relish.

"Really, really!" said the headmaster. "Indeed! This is—dear me! I shall certainly—They threw you in!—Yes, I shall—certainly——"

Encouraged by this appreciative reception of his story, Mr. Butt started it again, right from the beginning.

"I was on my beat, sir, and I thought I heard a disturbance. I says to myself, ''Allo,' I says, 'a frakkus. Lots of them all gathered together, and fighting.' I says, beginning to suspect something, 'Wot's this all about, I wonder?' I says. 'Blow me if I don't think it's a frakkus.' And," concluded Mr. Butt, with the air of one confiding a secret, "and it *was* a frakkus!"

"And these boys actually threw you into the pond?"

"*Plop*, sir! Mrs. Butt is drying my uniform at home at this very moment as we sit talking here, sir. She says to me, 'Why, whatever *'ave* you been a-doing? You're all wet.' And," he added, again with the confidential air, "I *was*, too. Wringin' wet."

The headmaster's frown deepened.

"And you are certain that your assailants were boys from the school?"

"Sure as I am that I'm sitting here, sir. They all 'ad their caps on their heads, sir."

"I have never heard of such a thing. I can hardly believe that it is possible. They actually seized you, and threw you into the water——"

"*Splish*, sir!" said the policeman, with a vividness of imagery both surprising and gratifying.

The headmaster tapped restlessly on the floor with his foot.

"How many boys were there?" he asked.

"Couple of 'undred, sir," said Mr. Butt promptly.

"Two hundred!"

"It was dark, sir, and I couldn't see not to say properly; but if you ask me my frank and private opinion I should say couple of 'undred."

"H'm—— Well, I will look into the matter at once. They shall be punished."

"Yes, sir."

"Ye-e-s—H'm—Yes—Most severely."

"Yes, sir."

"Yes—Thank you, constable. Good night."

"Good night, sir."

The headmaster of Wrykyn was not a motorist. Owing to this disadvantage he made a mistake. Had he been a motorist, he would have known that statements by the police in the matter of figures must be divided by any number from two to ten, according to discretion. As it was, he accepted Constable Butt's report almost as it stood. He thought that he might possibly have been mistaken as to the exact numbers of those concerned in his immersion; but he accepted the statement in so far as it indicated that the thing had been the work of a considerable section of the school, and not of only one or two individuals. And this made all the difference to his method of dealing with the affair. Had he known how few were the numbers of those responsible for the cold in the head which subsequently attacked Constable Butt, he would have asked for their names, and an extra lesson would have settled the entire matter.

As it was, however, he got the impression that the school, as a whole, was culpable, and he proceeded to punish the school as a whole.

It happened that, about a week before the pond episode, a certain member of the Royal Family had recovered from a dangerous illness. No official holiday had been given to the schools in honour of the recovery, but Eton and Harrow had set the example, which was followed throughout the kingdom, and Wrykyn had come into line with the rest. Only two days before the O.W.s matches the headmaster had given out a notice in the hall that the following Friday would be a whole holiday; and the school, always ready to stop work, had approved of the announcement exceedingly.

The step which the headmaster decided to take by way of avenging Mr. Butt's wrongs was to stop this holiday.

He gave out a notice to that effect on the Monday.

The school was thunderstruck. It could not understand it. The pond affair had, of course, become public property; and those who had had nothing to do with it had been much amused. "There'll be a frightful row about it," they had said, thrilled with the pleasant excitement of those who see trouble approaching and themselves looking on from a comfortable distance without risk or uneasiness. They were not malicious. They did not want to see their friends in difficulties. But there is no denying that a row does break the monotony of a school term. The thrilling feeling that something is going to happen is the salt of life. . . .

And here they were, right in it after all. The blow had fallen, and crushed guilty and innocent alike.

The school's attitude can be summed up in three words. It was one vast, blank, astounded "Here, I *say!*"

Everybody was saying it, though not always in those words. When condensed, everybody's comment on the situation came to that.

There is something rather pathetic in the indignation of a school. It must always, or nearly always, expend itself in words, and in private at that. Even the consolation of getting on to platforms and shouting at itself is denied to it. A public school has no Hyde Park.

There is every probability—in fact, it is certain—that, but for one malcontent, the school's indignation would have been allowed to simmer down in the usual way, and finally become a mere vague memory.

The malcontent was Wyatt. He had been responsible for the starting of the matter, and he proceeded now to carry it on till it blazed up into the biggest thing of its kind ever known at Wrykyn—the Great Picnic.

Anyone who knows the public schools, their iron-bound conservatism, and, as a whole, intense respect for order and authority, will appreciate the magnitude of his feat, even though he may not approve of it. Leaders of men are rare. Leaders of boys are almost unknown. It requires genius to sway a school.

It would be an absorbing task for a psychologist to trace the various stages by which an impossibility was changed into a reality. Wyatt's coolness and matter-of-fact determination were his chief weapons. His popularity and reputation for lawlessness helped him. A conversation which he had with Neville-Smith, a day-boy, is typical of the way in which he forced his point of view on the school.

Neville-Smith was thoroughly representative of the average Wrykynian. He could play his part in any minor "rag" which interested him, and probably considered himself, on the whole, a daring sort of person. But at heart he had an enormous respect for authority. Before he came to Wyatt, he would not have dreamed of proceeding beyond words in his revolt. Wyatt acted on him like some drug.

Neville-Smith came upon Wyatt on his way to the nets. The notice concerning the holiday had only been given out that morning, and he was full of it. He expressed his opinion of the headmaster freely and in well-chosen words. He said it was a swindle, that it was all rot, and that it was a beastly shame. He added that something ought to be done about it.

"What are you going to do?" asked Wyatt.

"Well," said Neville-Smith a little awkwardly, guiltily conscious that he had been frothing, and scenting sarcasm, "I don't suppose one can actually *do* anything."

"Why not?" said Wyatt.

"What do you mean?"

"Why don't you take the holiday?"

"What? Not turn up on Friday!"

"Yes. I'm not going to."

Neville-Smith stopped and stared. Wyatt was unmoved.

"You're what?"

"I simply shan't go to school."

"You're rotting."

"All right."

"No, but, I say, ragging barred. Are you just going to go off, though the holiday's been stopped?"

"That's the idea."

"You'll get sacked."

"I suppose so. But only because I shall be the only one to do it. If the whole school took Friday off, they couldn't do much. They couldn't sack the whole school."

"By Jove, nor could they! I say!"

They walked on, Neville-Smith's mind in a whirl, Wyatt whistling.

"I say," said Neville-Smith after a pause. "It would be a bit of a rag."

"Not bad."

"Do you think the chaps would do it?"

"If they understood they wouldn't be alone."

Another pause.

"Shall I ask some of them?" said Neville-Smith.

"Do."

"I could get quite a lot, I believe."

"That would be a start, wouldn't it? I could get a couple of dozen from Wain's. We should be forty or fifty strong to start with."

"I say, what a score, wouldn't it be?"

"Yes."

"I'll speak to the chaps tonight, and let you know."

"All right," said Wyatt. "Tell them that I shall be going anyhow. I should be glad of a little company."

.   .   .   .   .

The school turned in on the Thursday night in a restless, excited way. There were mysterious whisperings and gigglings. Groups kept forming in corners apart, to disperse casually and innocently on the approach of some person in authority.

An air of expectancy permeated each of the houses.

CHAPTER X

THE GREAT PICNIC

MORNING school at Wrykyn started at nine o'clock. At that hour there was a call-over in each of the form-rooms. After call-over the forms proceeded to the Great Hall for prayers.

A strangely desolate feeling was in the air at nine o'clock on the Friday morning. Sit in the grounds of a public school any afternoon in the summer holidays, and you will get exactly the same sensation of being alone in the world as came to the dozen or so day-boys who bicycled through the gates that morning. Wrykyn was a boarding-school for the most part, but it had its leaven of day-boys. The majority of these lived in the town, and walked to school. A few, however, whose homes were farther away, came on bicycles. One plutocrat did the journey in a motor-car, rather to the scandal of the authorities, who, though unable to interfere, looked askance when compelled by the warning toot of the horn to skip from road to pavement. A form-master has the strongest objection to being made to skip like a young ram by a boy to whom he has only the day before given a hundred lines for shuffling his feet in form.

It seemed curious to these cyclists that there should be nobody about. Punctuality is the politeness of princes, but it was not a leading characteristic of the school; and at three minutes to nine, as a general rule, you might see the gravel in front of the buildings freely dotted with sprinters, trying to get in in time to answer their names.

It was curious that there should be nobody about today.

A wave of reform could scarcely have swept through the houses during the night.

And yet—where was everybody?

Time only deepened the mystery. The form-rooms, like the gravel, were empty.

The cyclists looked at one another in astonishment. What could it mean?

It was an occasion on which sane people wonder if their brains are not playing them some unaccountable trick.

"I say," said Willoughby, of the Lower Fifth, to Brown, the only other occupant of the form-room, "the old man *did* stop the holiday today, didn't he?"

"Just what I was going to ask you," said Brown. "It's jolly rum. I distinctly remember him giving it out in the Hall that it was going to be stopped because of the O.W.s day row."

"So do I. I can't make it out. Where *is* everybody?"

"They can't *all* be late."

"Somebody would have turned up by now. Why, it's just striking."

"Perhaps he sent another notice round the houses late last night, saying it was on again all right. I say, what a swindle if he did. Someone might have let us know. I should have got up an hour later."

"So should I."

"Hullo, here *is* somebody."

It was the master of the Lower Fifth, Mr. Spence. He walked briskly into the room, as was his habit. Seeing the obvious void, he stopped in his stride, and looked puzzled.

"Willoughby. Brown. Are you the only two here? Where is everybody?"

"Please, sir, we don't know. We were just wondering."

"Have you seen nobody?"

"No, sir. We were just wondering, sir, if the holiday had been put on again, after all."

"I've heard nothing about it. I should have received some sort of intimation if it had been."

"Yes, sir."

"Do you mean to say that you have seen *nobody*, Brown?"

"Only about a dozen fellows, sir. The usual lot who come on bikes, sir."

"None of the boarders?"

"No, sir. Not a single one."

"This is extraordinary."

Mr. Spence pondered.

"Well," he said, "you two fellows had better go along up to the Hall. I shall go to the Common Room and make inquiries. Perhaps, as you say, there is a holiday today, and the notice was not brought to me."

Mr. Spence told himself, as he walked to the Common Room, that this might be a possible solution of the difficulty. He was not a house-master, and lived by himself in rooms in the town. It was just conceivable that they might have forgotten to tell him of the change in the arrangements.

But in the Common Room the same perplexity reigned. Half a dozen masters were seated round the room, and a few more were standing. And they were all very puzzled.

A brisk conversation was going on. Several voices hailed Mr. Spence as he entered.

"Hullo, Spence. Are you alone in the world too?"

"Any of your boys turned up, Spence?"

"You in the same condition as we are, Spence?"

Mr. Spence seated himself on the table.

"Haven't any of your fellows turned up, either?" he said.

"When I accepted the honourable post of Lower Fourth master in this abode of sin," said Mr. Seymour, "it was on the distinct understanding that there was going to *be* a Lower Fourth. Yet I go into my form-room this morning, and what do I find? Simply Emptiness, and Pickersgill II whistling 'The Lost Chord' all flat. I consider I have been hardly treated."

"I have no complaint to make against Brown and Willoughby, as individuals," said Mr. Spence; "but, considered as a form, I call them short measure."

"I confess that I am entirely at a loss," said Mr. Shields precisely. "I have never been confronted with a situation like this since I became a schoolmaster."

"It is most mysterious," agreed Mr. Wain, plucking at his beard. "Exceedingly so."

The younger masters, notably Mr. Spence and Mr. Seymour, had begun to look on the thing as a huge jest.

"We had better teach ourselves," said Mr. Seymour. "Spence, do a hundred lines for laughing in form."

The door burst open.

"Hullo, here's another scholastic Little Bo-Peep," said Mr. Seymour. "Well, Appleby, have you lost your sheep, too?"

"You don't mean to tell me——" began Mr. Appleby.

"I do," said Mr. Seymour. "Here we are, fifteen of us, all good men and true, graduates of our Universities, and, as far as I can see, if we divide up the boys who have come to school this morning on fair share-and-share-alike lines, it will work out at about two-thirds of a boy each. Spence, will you take a third of Pickersgill II?"

"I want none of your charity," said Mr. Spence loftily. "You don't seem to realize that I'm the best off of you all. I've got two in my form. It's no good offering me your Pickersgills. I simply haven't room for them."

"What does it all mean?" exclaimed Mr. Appleby.

"If you ask me," said Mr. Seymour, "I should say that it meant that the school, holding the sensible view that first thoughts are best, have ignored the head's change of mind, and are taking their holiday as per original programme."

"They surely cannot——!"

"Well, where are they then?"

"Do you seriously mean that the entire school has—has *rebelled*?"

"'Nay, sire,'" quoted Mr. Spence, "'a revolution!'"

"I never heard of such a thing!"

"We're making history," said Mr. Seymour.

"It will be rather interesting," said Mr. Spence, "to see how the head will deal with a situation like this. One can rely on him to do the statesmanlike thing, but I'm bound to say I shouldn't care to be in his place. It seems to me these boys hold all the cards. You can't expel a whole school. There's safety in numbers. The thing is colossal."

"It is deplorable," said Mr. Wain, with austerity. "Exceedingly so."

"I try to think so," said Mr. Spence, "but it's a struggle. There's a Napoleonic touch about the business that appeals to one. Disorder on a small scale is bad, but this is immense. I've never heard of anything like it at any public school. When I was at Winchester, my last year there, there was pretty nearly a revolution because the captain of cricket was expelled on the eve of the Eton match. I remember making inflammatory speeches myself on that occasion. But we stopped on the right side of the line. We were satisfied with growling. But this——!"

Mr. Seymour got up.

"It's an ill wind," he said. "With any luck we ought to get the day off, and it's ideal weather for a holiday. The head can hardly ask us to sit indoors, teaching nobody. If I have to stew in my form-room all day, instructing Pickersgill II, I shall make things exceedingly sultry for that youth. He will wish that the Pickersgill progeny had stopped short at his elder brother. He will not value life. In the meantime, as it's already ten past, hadn't we better be going up to the Hall to see what the orders of the day *are*?"

"Look at Shields," said Mr. Spence. "He might be posing for a statue to be called 'Despair!' He reminds me of Macduff. *Macbeth*, Act IV, somewhere near the end. 'What, all my pretty chickens, at one fell swoop?' That's what Shields is saying to himself."

"It's all very well to make a joke of it, Spence," said Mr. Shields querulously, "but it is most disturbing. Most."

"Exceedingly," agreed Mr. Wain.

The bereaved company of masters walked on up the stairs that led to the Great Hall.

CHAPTER XI

THE CONCLUSION OF THE PICNIC

IF the form-rooms had been lonely, the Great Hall was doubly, trebly, so. It was a vast room, stretching from side to side of the middle block, and its ceiling soared up into a distant dome. At one end was a dais and an organ, and at intervals down the room stood long tables. The panels were covered with the names of Wrykynians who had won scholarships at Oxford and Cambridge, and of Old Wrykynians who had taken firsts in Mods or Greats, or achieved any other recognized success, such as a place in the Indian Civil Service list. A silent testimony, these panels, to the work the school had done in the world.

Nobody knew exactly how many the Hall could hold, when packed to its fullest capacity. The six hundred odd boys at the school seemed to leave large gaps unfilled.

This morning there was a mere handful, and the place looked worse than empty.

The Sixth Form were there, and the school prefects. The Great Picnic had not affected their numbers. The Sixth stood by their table in a solid group. The other tables were occupied by ones and twos. A buzz of conversation was going on, which did not cease when the masters filed into the room and took their places. Everyone realized by this time that the biggest row in Wrykyn history was well under way; and the thing had to be discussed.

In the masters' library Mr. Wain and Mr. Shields, the spokesmen of the Common Room, were breaking the news to the headmaster.

The headmaster was a man who rarely betrayed emotion in his public capacity. He heard Mr. Shields's rambling remarks, punctuated by Mr. Wain's "Exceedinglys," to an end. Then he gathered up his cap and gown.

"You say that the whole school is absent?" he remarked quietly.

Mr. Shields, in a long-winded flow of words, replied that that was what he did say.

"Ah!" said the headmaster.

There was a silence.

"'M!" said the headmaster.

There was another silence.

"Ye—e—s!" said the headmaster.

He then led the way into the Hall.

Conversation ceased abruptly as he entered. The school, like an audience at a theatre when the hero has just appeared on the stage, felt that the serious interest of the drama had begun. There was a dead silence at every table as he strode up the room and on to the dais.

There was something titanic in his calmness. Every eye was on his face as he passed up the Hall, but not a sign of perturbation could the school read. To judge from his expression, he might have been unaware of the emptiness around him.

The master who looked after the music of the school, and incidentally accompanied the hymn with which prayers at Wrykyn opened, was waiting, puzzled, at the foot of the dais. It seemed improbable that things would go on as usual, and he did not know whether he was expected to be at the organ, or not. The headmaster's placid face reassured him. He went to his post.

The hymn began. It was a long hymn, and one which the school liked for its swing and noise. As a rule, when it was sung, the Hall re-echoed. Today, the thin sound of the voices had quite an uncanny effect. The organ boomed through the deserted room.

The school, or the remnants of it, waited impatiently while the prefect whose turn it was to read stammered nervously through the lesson. They were anxious to get on to what the Head was going to say at the end of prayers. At last it was over. The school waited, all ears.

The headmaster bent down from the dais and called to Firby-Smith, who was standing in his place with the Sixth.

The Gazeka, blushing warmly, stepped forward.

"Bring me a school list, Firby-Smith," said the headmaster.

The Gazeka was wearing a pair of very squeaky shoes that morning. They sounded deafening as he walked out of the room.

The school waited.

Presently a distant squeaking was heard, and Firby-Smith returned, bearing a large sheet of paper.

The headmaster thanked him, and spread it out on the reading-desk.

Then, calmly, as if it were an occurrence of every day, he began to call the roll.

"Abney."

No answer.

"Adams."

No answer.

"Allenby."

"Here, sir," from a table at the end of the room. Allenby was a prefect, in the Science Sixth.

The headmaster made a mark against his name with a pencil.

"Arkwright."

No answer.

He began to call the names more rapidly.

"Arlington. Arthur. Ashe. Aston."

"Here, sir," in a shrill treble from the rider in motor-cars.

The headmaster made another tick.

The list came to an end after what seemed to the school an unconscionable time, and he rolled up the paper again, and stepped to the edge of the dais.

"All boys not in the Sixth Form," he said, "will go to

their form-rooms and get their books and writing materials, and return to the Hall."

("Good work," murmured Mr. Seymour to himself. "Looks as if we should get that holiday after all.")

"The Sixth Form will go to their form-room as usual. I should like to speak to the masters for a moment."

He nodded dismissal to the school.

The masters collected on the dais.

"I find that I shall not require your services today," said the headmaster. "If you will kindly set the boys in your forms some work that will keep them occupied, I will look after them here. It is a lovely day," he added, with a smile, "and I am sure you will all enjoy yourselves a great deal more in the open air."

"That," said Mr. Seymour to Mr. Spence, as they went downstairs, "is what I call a genuine sportsman."

"My opinion neatly expressed," said Mr. Spence. "Come on the river. Or shall we put up a net, and have a knock?"

"River, I think. Meet you at the boat-house."

"All right. Don't be long."

"If every day were run on these lines, school-mastering wouldn't be such a bad profession. I wonder if one could persuade one's form to run amuck as a regular thing."

"Pity one can't. It seems to me the ideal state of things. Ensures the greatest happiness of the greatest number."

"I say! Suppose the school has gone up the river, too, and we meet them! What shall we do?"

"Thank them," said Mr. Spence, "most kindly. They've done us well."

The school had not gone up the river. They had marched in a solid body, with the school band at their head playing Sousa, in the direction of Worfield, a market town of some importance, distant about five miles. Of what they did and what the natives thought of it all, no very distinct records remain. The thing is a tradition on the countryside now, an event colossal and heroic, to be talked about in the tap-room of the village inn during the long winter evenings. The papers got hold of it, but were curiously misled as to the nature of the demonstration. This was the fault of the reporter on the staff of the *Worfield Intelligencer and Farmers' Guide*, who saw in the thing a legitimate "march-out," and, questioning a straggler as to the reason for the expedition and gathering foggily that the restoration to health of the Eminent Person was at the bottom of it, said so in his paper. And two days later, at about the time when Retribution had got seriously to work, the *Daily Mail* reprinted the account, with comments and elaborations, and headed it "Loyal Schoolboys." The writer said that great credit was due to the headmaster of Wrykyn for his ingenuity in devising and organizing so novel a thanksgiving celebration. And there was the usual conversation between "a rosy-cheeked lad of some sixteen summers" and "our representative," in which the rosy-cheeked one spoke most kindly of the headmaster, who seemed to be a warm personal friend of his.

The remarkable thing about the Great Picnic was its orderliness. Considering that five hundred and fifty boys were ranging the country in a compact mass, there was wonderfully little damage done to property. Wyatt's genius did not stop short at organizing the march. In addition, he arranged a system of officers which effectually controlled the animal spirits of the rank and file. The prompt and decisive way in which rioters were dealt with during the earlier stages of the business proved a wholesome lesson to others who would have wished to have gone and done likewise. A spirit of martial law reigned over the Great Picnic. And towards the end of the day fatigue kept the rowdy-minded quiet.

At Worfield the expedition lunched. It was not a market day, fortunately, or the confusion in the narrow streets would have been hopeless. On ordinary days Worfield was more or less deserted. It is astonishing that the resources of the little town were equal to satisfying the needs of the picnickers. They descended on the place like an army of locusts.

Wyatt, as generalissimo of the expedition, walked into the Grasshopper and Ant, the leading inn of the town.

"Anything I can do for you, sir?" inquired the landlord politely.

"Yes, please," said Wyatt, "I want lunch for five hundred and fifty."

That was the supreme moment in mine host's life. It was his big subject of conversation ever afterwards. He always told that as his best story, and he always ended with the words, "You could ha' knocked me down with a feather!"

The first shock over, the staff of the Grasshopper and Ant bustled about. Other inns were called upon for help. Private citizens rallied round with bread, jam, and apples. And the army lunched sumptuously.

In the early afternoon they rested, and as evening began to fall, the march home was started.

At the school, net practice was just coming to an end when, faintly, as the garrison of Lucknow heard the first skirl of the pipes of the relieving force, those on the grounds heard the strains of the school band and a murmur of many voices. Presently the sounds grew more distinct, and up the Wrykyn road came marching the vanguard of the column, singing the school song. They looked weary but cheerful.

As the army drew near to the school, it melted away little by little, each house claiming its representatives. At the school gates only a handful were left.

Bob Jackson, walking back to Donaldson's, met Wyatt at the gate, and gazed at him, speechless.

"Hullo," said Wyatt, "been to the nets? I wonder if there's time for a ginger-beer before the shop shuts."

CHAPTER XII

MIKE GETS HIS CHANCE

THE headmaster was quite bland and business-like about it all. There were no impassioned addresses from the dais. He did not tell the school that it ought to be ashamed of itself. Nor did he say that he should never have thought it of them. Prayers on the Saturday morning were marked by no unusual features. There was, indeed, a stir of excitement when he came to the edge of the dais, and cleared his throat as a preliminary to making an announcement. Now for it, thought the school.

This was the announcement:

"There has been an outbreak of chicken-pox in the town. All streets except the High Street will in consequence be out of bounds till further notice."

He then gave the nod of dismissal.

The school streamed downstairs, marvelling.

The less astute of the picnickers, unmindful of the homely proverb about hallooing before leaving the wood, were openly exulting. It seemed plain to them that the headmaster, baffled by the magnitude of the thing, had resolved to pursue the safe course of ignoring it altogether. To lie low is always a shrewd piece of tactics, and there seemed no reason why the Head should not have decided on it in the present instance.

Neville-Smith was among these premature rejoicers.

"I say," he chuckled, overtaking Wyatt in the cloisters, "this is all right, isn't it! He's funked it. I thought he would. Finds the job too big to tackle."

Wyatt was damping.

"My dear chap," he said, "it's not over yet by a long chalk. It hasn't started yet."

"What do you mean? Why didn't he say anything about it in the Hall, then?"

"Why should he? Have you ever had credit at a shop?"

"Of course I have. What do you mean? Why?"

"Well, they didn't send in the bill right away. But it came all right."

"Do you think he's going to do something then?"

"Rather. You wait."

Wyatt was right.

Between ten and eleven on Wednesdays and Saturdays old Bates, the school sergeant, used to copy out the names of those who were in extra lesson, and post them outside the school shop. The school inspected the list during the quarter to eleven interval.

Today, rushing to the shop for its midday bun, the school was aware of a vast sheet of paper where usually there was but a small one. They surged round it. Buns were forgotten. What was it?

Then the meaning of the notice flashed upon them. The headmaster had acted. This bloated document was the extra lesson list, swollen with names as a stream swells with rain. It was a comprehensive document. It left out little.

"The following boys will go in to extra lesson this afternoon and next Wednesday," it began. And "the following boys" numbered four hundred.

"Bates must have got writer's cramp," said Clowes, as he read the huge scroll.

Wyatt met Mike after school, as they went back to the house.

"Seen the 'extra' list?" he remarked. "None of the kids are in it, I notice. Only the bigger fellows. Rather a good thing. I'm glad you got off."

"Thanks," said Mike, who was walking a little stiffly.

"I don't know what you call getting off. It seems to me you're the chaps who got off."

"How do you mean?"

"*We* got tanned," said Mike ruefully.

"What!"

"Yes. Everybody below the Upper Fourth."

Wyatt roared with laughter.

"By Gad," he said, "he is an old sportsman. I never saw such a man. He lowers all records."

"Glad you think it funny. You wouldn't have if you'd been me. I was one of the first to get it. He was quite fresh."

"Sting?"

"Should think it did."

"Well, buck up. Don't break down."

"I'm not breaking down," said Mike indignantly.

"All right. I thought you weren't. Anyhow, you're better off than I am."

"An extra's nothing much," said Mike.

"It is when it happens to come on the same day as the M.C.C. match."

"Oh, by Jove! I forgot. That's next Wednesday, isn't it? You won't be able to play!"

"No."

"I say, what rot!"

"It is, rather. Still, nobody can say I didn't ask for it. If one goes out of one's way to beg and beseech the Old Man to put one in extra, it would be a little rough on him to curse him when he does it."

"I should be awfully sick, if it were me."

"Well, it isn't you, so you're all right. You'll probably get my place in the team."

Mike smiled dutifully at what he supposed to be a humorous sally.

"Or, rather, one of the places," continued Wyatt, who seemed to be sufficiently in earnest. "They'll put a bowler in instead of me. Probably Druce. But there'll be several vacancies. Let's see. Me. Adams. Ashe. Any more?

No, that's the lot. I should think they'd give you a chance."

"You needn't joke," said Mike uncomfortably. He had his day-dreams, like everybody else, and they always took the form of playing for the first eleven (and, incidentally, making a century in record time). To have to listen while the subject was talked about lightly made him hot and prickly all over.

"I'm not rotting," said Wyatt seriously, "I'll suggest it to Burgess tonight."

"You don't think there's any chance of it, really, do you?" said Mike awkwardly.

"I don't see why not? Buck up in the scratch game this afternoon. Fielding especially. Burgess is simply mad on fielding. I don't blame him either, especially as he's a bowler himself. He'd shove a man into the team like a shot, whatever his batting was like, if his fielding was something extra special. So you field like a demon this afternoon, and I'll carry on the good work in the evening."

"I say," said Mike, overcome, "it's awfully decent of you, Wyatt."

Billy Burgess, captain of Wrykyn cricket, was a genial giant, who seldom allowed himself to be ruffled. The present was one of the rare occasions on which he permitted himself that luxury. Wyatt found him in his study, shortly before lock-up, full of strange oaths, like the soldier in Shakespeare.

"You rotter! You rotter! You *worm*!" he observed crisply, as Wyatt appeared.

"Dear old Billy!" said Wyatt. "Come on, give me a kiss, and let's be friends."

"You——!"

"William! William!"

"If it wasn't illegal, I'd like to tie you and Ashe and that blackguard Adams up in a big sack, and drop you into the river. And I'd jump on the sack first. What do you mean by letting the team down like this? I know you were at the bottom of it all."

He struggled into his shirt—he was changing after a bath—and his face popped wrathfully out at the other end.

"I'm awfully sorry, Bill," said Wyatt. "The fact is, in the excitement of the moment the M.C.C. match went clean out of my mind."

"You haven't got a mind," grumbled Burgess. "You've got a cheap brown paper substitute. That's your trouble."

Wyatt turned the conversation tactfully.

"How many wickets did you get today?" he asked.

"Eight. For a hundred and three. I was on the spot. Young Jackson caught a hot one off me at third man. That kid's good."

"Why don't you play him against the M.C.C. on Wednesday?" said Wyatt, jumping at his opportunity.

"What? Are you sitting on my left shoe?"

"No. There it is in the corner."

"Right ho! . . . What were you saying?"

"Why not play young Jackson for the first?"

"Too small."

"Rot. What does size matter? Cricket isn't rugger. Besides, he isn't small. He's as tall as I am."

"I suppose he is. Dash, I've dropped my stud."

Wyatt waited patiently till he had retrieved it. Then he returned to the attack.

"He's as good a bat as his brother, and a better field."

"Old Bob can't field for toffee. I will say that for him. Dropped a sitter off me today. Why the deuce fellows can't hold catches when they drop slowly into their mouths I'm hanged if I can see."

"You play him," said Wyatt. "Just give him a trial. That kid's a genius at cricket. He's going to be better than any of his brothers, even Joe. Give him a shot."

Burgess hesitated.

"You know, it's a bit risky," he said. "With you three lunatics out of the team we can't afford to try many experiments. Better stick to the men at the top of the second."

Wyatt got up, and kicked the wall as a vent for his feelings.

"You rotter," he said. "Can't you *see* when you've got a good man? Here's this kid waiting for you ready-made with a style like Hutton's, and you rave about top men in the second, chaps who play forward at everything, and pat half-volleys back to the bowler! Do you realize that your only chance of being known to Posterity is as the man who gave M. Jackson his colours at Wrykyn? In a few years he'll be playing for England, and you'll think it a favour if he nods to you in the pav at Lord's. When you're a white-haired old man you'll go doddering about, gassing to your grandchildren, poor kids, how you 'discovered' M. Jackson. It'll be the only thing they'll respect you for."

Wyatt stopped for breath.

"All right," said Burgess, "I'll think it over. Frightful gift of the gab you've got, Wyatt."

"Good," said Wyatt. "Think it over. And don't forget what I said about the grandchildren. You would like little Wyatt Burgess and the other little Burgesses to respect you in your old age, wouldn't you? Very well, then. So long. The bell went ages ago. I shall be locked out."

On the Monday morning Mike passed the notice-board just as Burgess turned away from pinning up the list of the team to play the M.C.C. He read it, and his heart missed a beat. For, bottom but one, just above the W. B. Burgess, was a name that leaped from the paper at him. His own name.

CHAPTER XIII

THE M.C.C. MATCH

IF the day happens to be fine, there is a curious, dreamlike atmosphere about the opening stages of a first-eleven match. Everything seems hushed and expectant. The rest of the school have gone in after the interval at eleven o'clock, and you are alone on the ground with a cricket bag. The only signs of life are a few pedestrians on the road beyond the railings and one or two blazer and flannel-clad forms in the pavilion. The sense of isolation is trying to the nerves, and a school team usually bats twenty-five per cent better after lunch, when the strangeness has worn off.

Mike walked across from Wain's, where he had changed, feeling quite hollow. He could almost have cried with pure fright. Bob had shouted after him from a window as he passed Donaldson's, to wait, so that they could walk over together; but conversation was the last thing Mike desired at that moment.

He had almost reached the pavilion when one of the M.C.C. team came down the steps, saw him, and stopped dead.

"By Jove, Saunders!" cried Mike.

"Why, Master Mike!"

The professional beamed, and quite suddenly, the lost, hopeless feeling left Mike. He felt as cheerful as if he and Saunders had met in the meadow at home, and were just going to begin a little quiet net-practice.

"Why, Master Mike, you don't mean to say you're playing for the school already?"

Mike nodded happily.

"Isn't it terrific?" he said.

Saunders slapped his leg in a sort of ecstasy.

"Didn't I always say it, sir," he chuckled. "Wasn't I right? I used to say to myself it 'ud be a pretty good school team that 'ud leave you out."

"Of course, I'm only playing as a sub., you know. Three chaps are in extra, and I got one of the places."

"Well, you'll make a hundred today, Master Mike, and then they'll have to put you in."

"Wish I could!"

"Master Joe's come down with the Club," said Saunders.

"Joe! Has he really? How ripping! Hullo, here he is. Hullo, Joe?"

The greatest of all the Jacksons was descending the pavilion steps with the gravity befitting an All England batsman. He stopped short, as Saunders had done.

"Mike! You aren't playing!"

"Yes."

"Well, I'm hanged! Young marvel, isn't he, Saunders?"

"He is, sir," said Saunders. "Got all the strokes. I always said it, Master Joe. Only wants the strength."

Joe took Mike by the shoulder, and walked him off in the direction of a man in a Zingari blazer who was bowling slows to another of the M.C.C. team. Mike recognized him with awe as one of the three best amateur wicket-keepers in the country.

"What do you think of this?" said Joe, exhibiting Mike, who grinned bashfully. "Aged ten last birthday, and playing for the school. You *are* only ten, aren't you, Mike?"

"Brother of yours?" asked the wicket-keeper.

"Probably too proud to own the relationship, but he is."

"Isn't there any end to you Jacksons?" demanded the wicket-keeper in an aggrieved tone. "I never saw such a family."

"This is our star. You wait till he gets at us today. Saunders is our only bowler, and Mike's been brought up on Saunders. You'd better win the toss if you want a chance of getting a knock and lifting your average out of the minuses."

"I *have* won the toss," said the other with dignity. "Do you think I don't know the elementary duties of a captain?"

The school went out to field with mixed feelings. The wicket was hard and true, which would have made it pleasant to be going in first. On the other hand, they would feel decidedly better and fitter for centuries after the game had been in progress an hour or so. Burgess was glad as a private individual, sorry as a captain. For himself, the sooner he got hold of the ball and began to bowl the better he liked it. As a captain, he realized that a side with Joe Jackson in it, not to mention the other first-class men, was not a side to which he would have preferred to give away an advantage. Mike was feeling that by no possibility could he hold the simplest catch, and hoping that nothing would come his way. Bob, conscious of being an uncertain field, was feeling just the same.

The M.C.C. opened with Joe and a man in an Oxford Authentic cap. The beginning of the game was quiet. Burgess's yorker was nearly too much for the latter in the first over, but he contrived to chop it away, and the pair gradually settled down. At twenty, Joe began to open his shoulders. Twenty became forty with disturbing swiftness, and Burgess tried a change of bowling.

It seemed for one instant as if the move had been a success, for Joe, still taking risks, tried to late-cut a rising ball, and snicked it straight into Bob's hands at second slip. It was the easiest of slip-catches, but Bob fumbled it, dropped it, almost held it a second time, and finally let it fall miserably to the ground. It was a moment too painful for words. He rolled the ball back to the bowler in silence.

One of those weary periods followed when the batsman's

defence seems to the fieldsmen absolutely impregnable. There was a sickening inevitableness in the way in which every ball was played with the very centre of the bat. And, as usual, just when things seemed most hopeless, relief came. The Authentic, getting in front of his wicket, to pull one of the simplest long-hops ever seen on a cricket field, missed it, and was l.b.w. And the next ball upset the new-comer's leg stump.

The school revived. Bowlers and field were infused with a new life. Another wicket—two stumps knocked out of the ground by Burgess—helped the thing on. When the bell rang for the end of morning school, five wickets were down for a hundred and thirteen.

But from the end of school till lunch things went very wrong indeed. Joe was still in at one end, invincible; and at the other was the great wicket-keeper. And the pair of them suddenly began to force the pace till the bowling was in a tangled knot. Four after four, all round the wicket, with never a chance or a mishit to vary the monotony. Two hundred went up, and two hundred and fifty. Then Joe reached his century, and was stumped next ball. Then came lunch.

The rest of the innings was like the gentle rain after the thunderstorm. Runs came with fair regularity, but wickets fell at intervals, and when the wicket-keeper was run out at length for a lively sixty-three, the end was very near. Saunders, coming in last, hit two boundaries, and was then caught by Mike. His second hit had just lifted the M.C.C. total over the three hundred.

Three hundred is a score that takes some making on any ground, but on a fine day it was not an unusual total for the Wrykyn eleven. Some years before, against Ripton, they had run up four-hundred-and-sixteen; and only last season had massacred a very weak team of Old Wrykynians with a score that only just missed the fourth hundred.

Unfortunately, on the present occasion, there was scarcely time, unless the bowling happened to get completely collared, to make the runs. It was a quarter to four when the innings began, and stumps were to be drawn at a quarter to seven. A hundred an hour is quick work.

Burgess, however, was optimistic, as usual. "Better have a go for them," he said to Berridge and Marsh, the school first pair.

Following out this courageous advice, Berridge, after hitting three boundaries in his first two overs, was stumped half-way through the third.

After this, things settled down. Morris, the first-wicket man, was a thoroughly sound bat, a little on the slow side, but exceedingly hard to shift. He and Marsh proceeded to play themselves in, until it looked as if they were likely to stay till the drawing of stumps.

A comfortable, rather somnolent feeling settled upon the school. A long stand at cricket is a soothing sight to watch. There was an absence of hurry about the batsmen which harmonized well with the drowsy summer afternoon. And yet runs were coming at a fair pace. The hundred went up at five o'clock, the hundred and fifty at half-past. Both batsmen were completely at home, and the M.C.C. third-change bowlers had been put on.

Then the great wicket-keeper took off the pads and gloves, and the fieldsmen retired to posts at the extreme edge of the ground.

"Lobs," said Burgess. "By Jove, I wish I was in."

It seemed to be the general opinion among the members of the Wrykyn eleven on the pavilion balcony that Morris and Marsh were in luck. The team did not grudge them their good fortune, because they had earned it; but they were distinctly envious.

Lobs are the most dangerous, insinuating things in the world. Everybody knows in theory the right way to treat them. Everybody knows that the man who is content not to try to score more than a single cannot get out to them. Yet nearly everybody does get out to them.

It was the same story today. The first over yielded six runs, all through gentle taps along the ground. In the second, Marsh hit an over-pitched one along the ground to the terrace bank. The next ball he swept round to the leg boundary. And that was the end of Marsh. He saw himself scoring at the rate of twenty-four an over. Off the last ball he was stumped by several feet, having done himself credit by scoring seventy.

The long stand was followed, as usual, by a series of disasters. Marsh's wicket had fallen at a hundred and eighty. Ellerby left at a hundred and eighty-six. By the time the scoring-board registered two hundred, five wickets were down, three of them victims to the lobs. Morris was still in at one end. He had refused to be tempted. He was jogging on steadily to his century.

Bob Jackson went in next, with instructions to keep his eye on the lob-man.

For a time things went well. Saunders, who had gone on to bowl again after a rest, seemed to give Morris no trouble, and Bob put him through the slips with apparent ease. Twenty runs were added, when the lob-bowler once more got in his deadly work. Bob, letting alone a ball wide of the off-stump under the impression that it was going to break away, was disagreeably surprised to find it break in instead, and hit the wicket. The bowler smiled sadly, as if he hated to have to do these things.

Mike's heart jumped as he saw the bails go. It was his turn next.

"Two hundred and twenty-nine," said Burgess, "and it's ten past six. No good trying for the runs now. Stick in," he added to Mike. "That's all you've got to do."

All! . . . Mike felt as if he was being strangled. His heart was racing like the engines of a motor. He knew his teeth were chattering. He wished he could stop them. What a time Bob was taking to get back to the pavilion! He wanted to rush out, and get the thing over.

At last he arrived, and Mike, fumbling at a glove, tottered out into the sunshine. He heard miles and miles away a sound of clapping, and a thin, shrill noise as if somebody were screaming in the distance. As a matter of fact, several members of his form and of the junior day-room at Wain's nearly burst themselves at that moment.

At the wickets, he felt better. Bob had fallen to the last ball of the over, and Morris, standing ready for Saunders's delivery, looked so calm and certain of himself that it was impossible to feel entirely without hope and self-confidence. Mike knew that Morris had made ninety-eight, and he supposed that Morris knew that he was very near his century; yet he seemed to be absolutely undisturbed. Mike drew courage from his attitude.

Morris pushed the first ball away to leg. Mike would have liked to have run two, but short leg had retrieved the ball as he reached the crease.

The moment had come, the moment which he had experienced only in dreams. And in the dreams he was always full of confidence, and invariably hit a boundary. Sometimes a drive, sometimes a cut, but always a boundary.

"To leg, sir," said the umpire.

"Don't be in a funk," said a voice. "Play straight, and you can't get out."

It was Joe, who had taken the gloves when the wicket-keeper went on to bowl.

Mike grinned, wryly but gratefully.

Saunders was beginning his run. It was all so home-like that for a moment Mike felt himself again. How often he had seen those two little skips and the jump. It was like being in the paddock again, with Marjory and the dogs waiting by the railings to fetch the ball if he made a drive.

Saunders ran to the crease, and bowled.

Now, Saunders was a conscientious man, and, doubtless, bowled the very best ball that he possibly could. On the other hand, it was Mike's first appearance for the school, and Saunders, besides being conscientious, was undoubtedly kind-hearted. It is useless to speculate as to whether he was trying to bowl his best that ball. If so, he failed signally. It was a half-volley, just the right distance away from the off-stump; the sort of ball Mike was wont to send nearly through the net at home. . . .

The next moment the dreams had come true. The umpire was signalling to the scoring-box, the school was shouting, extra-cover was trotting to the boundary to fetch the ball, and Mike was blushing and wondering whether it was bad form to grin.

From that ball onwards all was for the best in this best of all possible worlds. Saunders bowled no more half-volleys; but Mike played everything that he did bowl. He met the lobs with a bat like a barn-door. Even the departure of Morris, caught in the slips off Saunders's next over for a chanceless hundred and five, did not disturb him. All nervousness had left him. He felt equal to the situation. Burgess came in, and began to hit out as if he meant to knock off the runs. The bowling became a shade loose. Twice he was given full tosses to leg, which he hit to the terrace bank. Half-past six chimed, and two hundred and fifty went up on the telegraph board. Burgess continued to hit. Mike's whole soul was concentrated on keeping up his wicket. There was only Reeves to follow him, and Reeves was a victim to the first straight ball. Burgess had to hit because it was the only game he knew; but he himself must simply stay in.

The hands of the clock seemed to have stopped. Then suddenly he heard the umpire say "Last over," and he settled down to keep those six balls out of his wicket.

The lob-bowler had taken himself off, and the Oxford Authentic had gone on, fast left-hand.

The first ball was short and wide of the off-stump. Mike let it alone. Number two: yorker. Got him! Three: straight half-volley. Mike played it back to the bowler. Four: beat him, and missed the wicket by an inch. Five: another yorker. Down on it again in the old familiar way.

All was well. The match was a draw now whatever happened to him. He hit out, almost at a venture, at the last ball, and mid-off, jumping, just failed to reach it. It

92

hummed over his head, and ran like a streak along the turf and up the bank, and a great howl of delight went up from the school as the umpire took off the bails.

Mike walked away from the wicket with Joe and the wicket-keeper.

"I'm sorry about your nose, Joe," said the wicket-keeper in tones of grave solicitude.

"What's wrong with it?"

"At present," said the wicket-keeper, "nothing. But in a few years I'm afraid it's going to be put badly out of joint."

CHAPTER XIV

A SLIGHT IMBROGLIO

Mike got his third eleven colours after the M.C.C. match. As he had made twenty-three not out in a crisis in a first-eleven match, this may not seem an excessive reward. But it was all that he expected. One had to take the rungs of the ladder singly at Wrykyn. First one was given one's third-eleven cap. That meant, "You are a promising man, and we have our eye on you." Then came the second colours. They might mean anything from "Well, here you *are*. You won't get any higher, so you may as well have the thing now," to "This is just to show that we still have our eye on you."

Mike was a certainty now for the second. But it needed more than one performance to secure the first cap.

"I told you so," said Wyatt, naturally, to Burgess after the match.

"He's not bad," said Burgess. "I'll give him another shot."

But Burgess, as has been pointed out, was not a person who ever became gushing with enthusiasm.

So Wilkins, of the School House, who had played twice for the first eleven, dropped down into the second, as many a good man had done before him, and Mike got his place in the next match, against the Gentlemen of the County. Unfortunately for him, the visiting team, however gentlemanly, were not brilliant cricketers, at any rate as far as bowling was concerned. The school won the toss, went in first, and made three hundred and sixteen for five wickets, Morris making another placid century. The innings was declared closed before Mike had a chance of distinguishing himself. In an innings which lasted for one over he made two runs, not out; and had to console himself for the cutting short of his performance by the fact that his average for the school was still infinity. Bob, who was one of those lucky enough to have an unabridged innings, did better in this match, making twenty-five. But with Morris making a hundred and seventeen, and Berridge, Ellerby, and Marsh all passing the half-century, this score did not show up excessively.

We now come to what was practically a turning-point in Mike's career at Wrykyn. There is no doubt that his meteor-like flights at cricket had an unsettling effect on him. He was enjoying life amazingly, and, as is not uncommon with the prosperous, he waxed fat and kicked. Fortunately for him—though he did not look upon it in that light at the time—he kicked the one person it was most imprudent to kick. The person he selected was Firby-Smith. With anybody else the thing might have blown over, to the detriment of Mike's character; but Firby-Smith, having the most tender affection for his dignity, made a fuss.

It happened in this way. The immediate cause of the disturbance was a remark of Mike's, but the indirect cause was the unbearably patronizing manner which the head of Wain's chose to adopt towards him. The fact that he was playing for the school seemed to make no difference at all. Firby-Smith continued to address Mike merely as the small boy.

The following, *verbatim*, was the tactful speech which he addressed to him on the evening of the M.C.C. match, having summoned him to his study for the purpose.

"Well," he said, "you played a very decent innings this afternoon, and I suppose you're frightfully pleased with yourself, eh? Well, mind you don't go getting swelled head. See? That's all. Run along."

Mike departed, bursting with fury.

The next link in the chain was forged a week after the Gentlemen of the County match. House matches had begun, and Wain's were playing Appleby's. Appleby's made a hundred and fifty-odd, shaping badly for the most part against Wyatt's slows. Then Wain's opened their innings. The Gazeka, as head of the house, was captain of the side, and he and Wyatt went in first. Wyatt made a few mighty hits, and was then caught at cover. Mike went in first wicket.

For some ten minutes all was peace. Firby-Smith scratched away at his end, getting here and there a single and now and then a two, and Mike settled down at once to play what he felt was going to be the innings of a lifetime. Appleby's bowling was on the feeble side, with Raikes, of the third eleven, as the star, supported by some small change. Mike pounded it vigorously. To one who had been brought up on Saunders, Raikes possessed few subtleties. He had made seventeen, and was thoroughly set, when the Gazeka, who had the bowling, hit one in the direction of cover-point. With a certain type of batsman a single is a thing to take big risks for. And the Gazeka badly wanted that single.

"Come on," he shouted, prancing down the pitch.

Mike, who had remained in his crease with the idea that nobody even moderately sane would attempt a run for a hit like that, moved forward in a startled and irresolute manner. Firby-Smith arrived, shouting "Run!" and, cover having thrown the ball in, the wicket-keeper removed the bails.

These are solemn moments.

The only possibly way of smoothing over an episode of this kind is for the guilty man to grovel.

Firby-Smith did not grovel.

"Easy run there, you know," he said reprovingly.

The world swam before Mike's eyes. Through the red mist he could see Firby-Smith's face. The sun glinted on his rather prominent teeth. To Mike's distorted vision it seemed that the criminal was amused.

"Don't *laugh*, you grinning ape!" he cried. "It isn't funny."

He then made for the trees where the rest of the team were sitting.

Now Firby-Smith not only possessed rather prominent teeth; he was also sensitive on the subject. Mike's shaft sank in deeply. The fact that emotion caused him to swipe at a straight half-volley, miss it, and be bowled next ball made the wound rankle.

He avoided Mike on his return to the trees. And Mike, feeling now a little apprehensive, avoided him.

The Gazeka brooded apart for the rest of the afternoon, chewing the insult. At close of play he sought Burgess.

Burgess, besides being captain of the eleven was also head of the school. He was the man who arranged prefects' meetings. And only a prefects' meeting, thought Firby-Smith, could adequately avenge his lacerated dignity.

"I want to speak to you, Burgess," he said.

"What's up?" said Burgess.

"You know young Jackson in our house."

"What about him?"

"He's been frightfully insolent."

"Cheeked you?" said Burgess, a man of simple speech.

"I want you to call a prefects' meeting, and lick him."

Burgess looked incredulous.

"Rather a large order, a prefects' meeting," he said. "It has to be a pretty serious sort of thing for that."

"Frightful cheek to a school prefect *is* a serious thing," said Firby-Smith, with the air of one uttering an epigram.

"Well, I suppose—— What did he say to you?"

Firby-Smith related the painful details.

Burgess started to laugh, but turned the laugh into a cough.

"Yes," he said meditatively. "Rather thick. Still, I mean—— A prefects' meeting. Rather like crushing a thingummy with a what-d'you-call-it. Besides, he's a decent kid."

"He's frightfully conceited."

"Oh, well—— Well, anyhow, look here, I'll think it over, and let you know tomorrow. It's not the sort of thing to rush through without thinking about it."

And the matter was left temporarily at that.

CHAPTER XV

MIKE CREATES A VACANCY

Burgess walked off the ground feeling that fate was not using him well.

Here was he, a well-meaning youth who wanted to be on good terms with all the world, being jockeyed into slaughtering a kid whose batting he admired and whom personally he liked. And the worst of it was that he sympathized with Mike. He knew what it felt like to be run out just when one had got set, and he knew exactly how maddening the Gazeka's manner would be on such an occasion. On the other hand, officially he was bound to support the head of Wain's. Prefects must stand together or chaos will come.

He thought he would talk it over with somebody. Bob occurred to him. It was only fair that Bob should be told, as the nearest of kin.

And here was another grievance against fate. Bob was a person he did not particularly wish to see just then. For that morning he had posted up the list of the team to play for the school against Geddington, one of the four schools which Wrykyn met at cricket; and Bob's name did not appear on that list. Several things had contributed to that melancholy omission. In the first place, Geddington, to judge from the weekly reports in the *Sportsman* and *Field*, were strong this year at batting. In the second place, the results of the last few matches, and particularly the M.C.C. match, had given Burgess the idea that Wrykyn was weak at bowling. It became necessary, therefore, to drop a batsman out of the team in favour of a bowler. And either Mike or Bob must be the man.

Burgess was as rigidly conscientious as the captain of a school eleven should be. Bob was one of his best friends, and he would have given much to be able to put him in the team; but he thought the thing over, and put the temptation sturdily behind him. At batting there was not much to choose between the two, but in fielding there was a great deal. Mike was good. Bob was bad. So out Bob had gone, and Neville-Smith, a fair fast bowler at all times and on his day dangerous, took his place.

These clashings of public duty with private inclination are the drawbacks to the despotic position of captain of cricket at a public school. It is awkward having to meet your best friend after you have dropped him from the team, and it is difficult to talk to him as if nothing had happened.

Burgess felt very self-conscious as he entered Bob's study, and was rather glad that he had a topic of conversation ready to hand.

"Busy, Bob?" he asked.

"Hullo," said Bob, with a cheerfulness rather overdone in his anxiety to show Burgess, the man, that he did not hold him responsible in any way for the distressing acts of Burgess, the captain. "Take a pew. Don't these studies get beastly hot this weather. There's some ginger-beer in the cupboard. Have some?"

"No, thanks. I say, Bob, look here, I want to see you."

"Well, you can, can't you? This is me, sitting over here. The tall, dark, handsome chap."

"It's awfully awkward, you know," continued Burgess gloomily; "that ass of a young brother of yours——Sorry, but he *is* an ass, though he's your brother——"

"Thanks for the 'though,' Billy. You know how to put a thing nicely. What's Mike been up to?"

"It's that old fool the Gazeka. He came to me frothing with rage, and wanted me to call a prefects' meeting and touch young Mike up."

Bob displayed interest and excitement for the first time.

"Prefects' meeting! What the dickens is up? What's he been doing? Smith must be drunk. What's all the row about?"

Burgess repeated the main facts of the case as he had them from Firby-Smith.

"Personally, I sympathize with the kid," he added. "Still, the Gazeka *is* a prefect——"

Bob gnawed a pen-holder morosely.

"Silly young idiot," he said.

"Sickening thing being run out," suggested Burgess. "Still——"

"I know. It's rather hard to see what to do. I suppose if the Gazeka insists, one's bound to support him."

"I suppose so."

"Awful rot. Prefects' lickings aren't meant for that sort of thing. They're supposed to be for kids who steal buns at the shop or muck about generally. Not for a chap who curses a fellow who runs him out. I tell you what, there's just a chance Firby-Smith won't press the thing. He hadn't had time to get over it when he saw me. By now he'll have simmered down a bit. Look here, you're a pal of his, aren't you? Well, go and ask him to drop the business. Say you'll curse your brother and make him apologize, and that I'll kick him out of the team for the Geddington match."

It was a difficult moment for Bob. One cannot help one's thoughts, and for an instant the idea of going to Geddington with the team, as he would certainly do if Mike did not play, made him waver. But he recovered himself.

"Don't do that," he said. "I don't see there's a need for anything of that sort. You must play the best side you've got. I can easily talk the old Gazeka over. He gets all right in a second if he's treated the right way. I'll go and do it now."

Burgess looked miserable.

"I say, Bob," he said.

"Yes?"

"Oh, nothing—I mean, you're not a bad sort." With

which glowing eulogy he dashed out of the room, thanking his stars that he had won through a confoundly awkward business.

Bob went across to Wain's to interview and soothe Firby-Smith.

He found that outraged hero sitting moodily in his study like Achilles in his tent.

Seeing Bob, he became all animation.

"Look here," he said, "I wanted to see you. You know, that frightful young brother of yours——"

"I know, I know," said Bob. "Burgess was telling me. He wants kicking."

"He wants a frightful licking from the prefects," amended the aggrieved party.

"Well, I don't know, you know. Not much good lugging the prefects into it, is there? I mean, apart from everything else, not much of a catch for me, would it be, having to sit there and look on. I'm a prefect, too, you know."

Firby-Smith looked a little blank at this. He had a great admiration for Bob.

"I didn't think of you," he said.

"I thought you hadn't," said Bob. "You see it now, though, don't you?"

Firby-Smith returned to the original grievance.

"Well, you know, it was frightful cheek."

"Of course it was. Still, I think if I saw him and cursed him, and sent him up to you to apologize—— How would that do?"

"All right. After all, I did run him out."

"Yes, there's that, of course. Mike's all right, really. It isn't as if he did that sort of thing as a habit."

"No. All right then."

"Thanks," said Bob, and went to find Mike.

The lecture on deportment which he read that future All-England batsman in a secluded passage near the junior day-room left the latter rather limp and exceedingly meek.

For the moment all the jauntiness and exuberance had been drained out of him. He was a punctured balloon. Reflection, and the distinctly discouraging replies of those experts in school law to whom he had put the question, "What d'you think he'll do?" had induced a very chastened frame of mind.

He perceived that he had walked very nearly into a hornets' nest, and the realization of his escape made him agree readily to all the conditions imposed. The apology to the Gazeka was made without reserve, and the offensively forgiving, say-no-more-about-it-but-take-care-in-future air of the head of the house roused no spark of resentment in him, so subdued was his fighting spirit. All he wanted was to get the thing done with. He was not inclined to be critical.

And, most of all, he felt grateful to Bob. Firby-Smith, in the course of his address, had not omitted to lay stress on the importance of Bob's intervention. But for Bob, he gave him to understand, he, Mike, would have been prosecuted with the utmost rigour of the law. Mike came away with a confused picture in his mind of a horde of furious prefects bent on his slaughter, after the manner of a stage "excited crowd," and Bob waving them back. He realized that Bob had done him a good turn. He wished he could find some way of repaying him.

Curiously enough, it was an enemy of Bob's who suggested the way—Burton, of Donaldson's. Burton was a slippery young gentleman, fourteen years of age, who had frequently come into contact with Bob in the house, and owed him many grudges. With Mike he had always tried to form an alliance, though without success.

He happened to meet Mike going to school next morning, and unburdened his soul to him. It chanced that Bob and he had had another small encounter immediately after breakfast, and Burton felt revengeful.

"I say," said Burton, "I'm jolly glad you're playing for the first against Geddington."

"Thanks," said Mike.

"I'm specially glad for one reason."

"What's that?" inquired Mike, without interest.

"Because your beast of a brother has been chucked out. He'd have been playing but for you."

At any other time Mike would have heard Bob called a beast without active protest. He would have felt that it was no business of his to fight his brother's battles for him. But on this occasion he deviated from his rule.

He kicked Burton. Not once or twice, but several times, so that Burton, retiring hurriedly, came to the conclusion that it must be something in the Jackson blood, some taint, as it were. They were *all* beasts.

Mike walked on, weighing this remark, and gradually made up his mind. It must be remembered that he was in a confused mental condition, and that the only thing he realized clearly was that Bob had pulled him out of an uncommonly nasty hole. It seemed to him that it was necessary to repay Bob. He thought the thing over more fully during school, and his decision remained unaltered.

On the evening before the Geddington match, just before lock-up, Mike tapped at Burgess's study door. He tapped with his right hand, for his left was in a sling.

"Come in!" yelled the captain. "Hullo!"

"I'm awfully sorry, Burgess," said Mike. "I've crocked my wrist a bit."

"How did you do that? You were all right at the nets?"

"Slipped as I was changing," said Mike stolidly.

"Is it bad?"

"Nothing much. I'm afraid I shan't be able to play to-morrow."

"I say, that's bad luck. Beastly bad luck. We wanted your batting, too. Be all right, though, in a day or two, I suppose?"

"Oh, yes, rather."

"Hope so, anyway."

"Thanks. Good night."

"Good night."

And Burgess, with the comfortable feeling that he had managed to combine duty and pleasure after all, wrote a note to Bob at Donaldson's telling him to be ready to start with the team for Geddington by the eight-fifty-four next morning.

CHAPTER XVI

AN EXPERT EXAMINATION

MIKE'S Uncle John was a wanderer on the face of the earth. He had been an army surgeon in the days of his youth, and, after an adventurous career, mainly on the North-West Frontier, had inherited enough money to keep him in comfort for the rest of his life. He had thereupon left the service, and now spent most of his time flitting from one spot of Europe to another. He had been dashing up to Scotland on the day when Mike first became a Wrykynian, but a few weeks in an uncomfortable hotel in Skye and a few days in a comfortable one in Edinburgh had left him with the impression that he had now seen all that there was to be seen in North Britain and might reasonably shift his camp again.

Coming south, he had looked in on Mike's people for a brief space, and, at the request of Mike's mother, took the early express to Wrykyn in order to pay a visit of inspection.

His telegram arrived during morning school. Mike went down to the station to meet him after lunch.

Uncle John took command of the situation at once.

"School playing anybody today, Mike? I want to see a match."

"They're playing Geddington. Only it's away. There's a second match on."

"Why aren't you—— Hullo, I didn't see. What have you been doing to yourself?"

"Crocked my wrist a bit. It's nothing much."

"How did you do that?"

"Slipped while I was changing after cricket."

"Hurt?"

"Not much, thanks."

"Doctor seen it?"

"No. But it's really nothing. Be all right by Monday."

"H'm. Somebody ought to look at it. I'll have a look later on."

Mike did not appear to relish this prospect.

"It isn't anything, Uncle John, really. It doesn't matter a bit."

"Never mind. It won't do any harm having somebody examine it who knows a bit about these things. Now, what shall we do? Go on the river?"

"I shouldn't be able to steer."

"I could manage about that. Still, I think I should like to see the place first. Your mother's sure to ask me if you showed me round. It's like going over the stables when you're stopping at a country house. Got to be done, and better do it as soon as possible."

It is never very interesting playing the part of showman at school. Both Mike and his uncle were inclined to scamp the business. Mike pointed out the various landmarks without much enthusiasm—it is only after one has left a few years that the school buildings take to themselves romance—and Uncle John said, "Ah yes, I see. Very nice," two or three times in an absent voice; and they passed on to the cricket field, where the second eleven were playing a neighbouring engineering school. It was a glorious day. The sun had never seemed to Mike so bright or the grass so green. It was one of those days when the ball looks like a large vermilion-coloured football as it leaves the bowler's hand. If ever there was a day when it seemed to Mike that a century would have been a certainty, it was this Saturday. A sudden, bitter realization of all he had given up swept over him, but he choked the feeling down. The thing was done, and it was no good brooding over the might-have-beens now. Still—— And the Geddington ground was supposed to be one of the easiest scoring grounds of all the public schools!

"Well hit, by George!" remarked Uncle John, as Trevor, who had gone in first wicket for the second eleven, swept a half-volley to leg round to the bank where they were sitting.

"That's Trevor," said Mike. "Chap in Donaldson's. The fellow at the other end is Wilkins. He's in the School House. They look as if they were getting set. By Jove," he said enviously, "pretty good fun batting on a day like this."

Uncle John detected the envious note.

"I suppose you would have been playing here but for your wrist?"

"No, I was playing for the first."

"For the first? For the school! My word, Mike, I didn't know that. No wonder you're feeling badly treated. Of course, I remember your father saying you had played once for the school, and done well; but I thought that was only as a substitute. I didn't know you were a regular member of the team. What bad luck! Will you get another chance?"

"Depends on Bob."

"Has Bob got your place?"

Mike nodded.

"If he does well today, they'll probably keep him in."

"Isn't there room for both of you?"

"Such a lot of old colours. There are only three vacancies, and Henfrey got one of those a week ago. I expect they'll give one of the other two to a bowler, Neville-Smith, I should think, if he does well against Geddington. Then there'll be only the last place left."

"Rather awkward, that."

"Still, it's Bob's last year. I've got plenty of time. But I wish I could get in this year."

After they had watched the match for an hour, Uncle John's restless nature asserted itself.

"Suppose we go for a pull on the river now?" he suggested.

They got up.

"Let's just call at the shop," said Mike. "There ought to be a telegram from Geddington by this time. I wonder how Bob's got on."

Apparently Bob had not had a chance yet of distinguishing himself. The telegram read, "Geddington 151 for four. Lunch."

"Not bad that," said Mike. "But I believe they're weak in bowling."

They walked down the road towards the school landing-stage.

"The worst of a school," said Uncle John, as he pulled upstream with strong, unskilful stroke, "is that one isn't allowed to smoke on the grounds. I badly want a pipe. The next piece of shade that you see, sing out, and we'll put in there."

"Pull your left," said Mike. "That willow's what you want."

Uncle John looked over his shoulder, caught a crab, recovered himself, and steered the boat in under the shade of the branches.

"Put the rope over that stump. Can you manage with one hand? Here, let me—— Done it? Good. A-ah!"

He blew a great cloud of smoke into the air, and sighed contentedly.

"I hope you don't smoke, Mike?"

"No."

"Rotten trick for a boy. When you get to my age you need it. Boys ought to be thinking about keeping themselves fit and being good at games. Which reminds me. Let's have a look at the wrist."

A hunted expression came into Mike's eyes.

"It's really nothing," he began, but his uncle had already removed the sling, and was examining the arm with the neat rapidity of one who has been brought up to such things.

To Mike it seemed as if everything in the world was standing still and waiting. He could hear nothing but his own breathing.

His uncle pressed the wrist gingerly once or twice, then gave it a little twist.

"That hurt?" he asked.

"Ye—no," stammered Mike.

Uncle John looked up sharply. Mike was crimson.

"What's the game?" inquired Uncle John.

Mike said nothing.

There was a twinkle in his uncle's eyes.

"May as well tell me. I won't give you away. Why this wounded warrior business when you've no more the matter with you than I have?"

Mike hesitated.

"I only wanted to get out of having to write this morning. There was an exam on."

The idea had occurred to him just before he spoke. It had struck him as neat and plausible.

To Uncle John it did not appear in the same light.

"Do you always write with your left hand? And if you had gone with the first eleven to Geddington, wouldn't that have got you out of your exam? Try again."

When in doubt, one may as well tell the truth. Mike told it.

"I know. It wasn't that, really. Only——"

"Well?"

"Oh, well, dash it all then. Old Bob got me out of an awful row the day before yesterday, and he seemed a bit sick at not playing for the first, so I thought I might as well let him. That's how it *was*. Look here, swear you won't tell him."

Uncle John was silent. Inwardly he was deciding that the five shillings which he had intended to bestow on Mike on his departure should become a pound. (This, it may be mentioned as an interesting biographical fact, was the only occasion in his life on which Mike earned money at the rate of fifteen shillings a half-minute.)

"Swear you won't tell him. He'd be most frightfully sick if he knew."

"I won't tell him."

Conversation dwindled to vanishing-point. Uncle John smoked on in weighty silence, while Mike, staring up at the blue sky through the branches of the willow, let his mind wander to Geddington, where his fate was even now being sealed. How had the school got on? What had Bob done? If he made about twenty, would they give him his cap? Supposing . . .

A faint snore from Uncle John broke in on his meditations. Then there was a clatter as a briar pipe dropped on to the floor of the boat, and his uncle sat up, gaping.

"Jove, I was nearly asleep. What's the time? Just on six? Didn't know it was so late."

"I ought to be getting back soon, I think. Lock-up's at half past."

"Up with the anchor, then. You can tackle that rope with two hands now, eh? We are not observed. Don't fall overboard. I'm going to shove her off."

"There'll be another telegram, I should think," said Mike, as they reached the school gates.

"Shall we go and look?"

They walked to the shop.

A second piece of grey paper had been pinned up under the first. Mike pushed his way through the crowd. It was a longer message this time.

It ran as follows:

"Geddington 247 (Burgess six wickets, Neville-Smith four). Wrykyn 270 for nine (Berridge 86, Marsh 58, Jackson 48)."

Mike worked his way back through the throng, and rejoined his uncle.

"Well?" said Uncle John.

"We won."

He paused for a moment.

"Bob made forty-eight," he added carelessly.

Uncle John felt in his pocket, and silently slid a pound into Mike's hand.

It was the only possible reply.

CHAPTER XVII

ANOTHER VACANCY

WYATT got back late that night, arriving at the dormitory as Mike was going to bed.

"By Jove, I'm done," he said. "It was simply baking at Geddington. And I came back in a carriage with Neville-Smith and Ellerby, and they ragged the whole time. I wanted to go to sleep, only they wouldn't let me. Old Smith was awfully bucked because he'd taken four wickets. I should think he'd go off his nut if he took eight ever. He was singing comic songs when he wasn't trying to put Ellerby under the seat. How's your wrist?"

"Oh, better, thanks."

Wyatt began to undress.

"Any colours?" asked Mike after a pause. First eleven colours were generally given in the pavilion after a match or on the journey home.

"No. Only one or two thirds. Jenkins and Clephane, and another chap, can't remember who. No first, though."

"What was Bob's innings like?"

"Not bad. A bit lucky. He ought to have been out before he'd scored, and he *was* out when he'd made about sixteen, only the umpire didn't seem to know the l.b.w. rule. Never saw a clearer case in my life. I was in at the other end. Bit rotten for the Geddington chaps. Just lost them the match. Their umpire, too. Bit of luck for Bob. He didn't give the ghost of a chance after that."

"I should have thought they'd have given him his colours."

"Most captains would have done, only Burgess is so keen on fielding that he rather keeps off it."

"Why, did he field badly?"

"Rottenly. And the man always will choose Billy's bowling to drop catches off. And Billy would cut his rich uncle from Australia if he kept on dropping them off him. Bob's fielding's perfectly sinful. He was pretty bad at the beginning of the season, but now he's got so nervous that he's a dozen times worse. He turns a delicate green when he sees a catch coming. He let their best man off twice in one over, off Billy, today; and the chap went on and made a hundred odd. Ripping innings bar those two chances. I hear he's got an average of eighty in school matches this season. Beastly man to bowl to. Knocked me off in half a dozen overs. And, when he does give a couple of easy chances, Bob puts them both on the floor. Billy wouldn't have given him his cap after the match if he'd made a hundred. Bob's the sort of man who wouldn't catch a ball if you handed it to him on a plate, with water-cress round it."

Burgess, reviewing the match that night, as he lay awake in his cubicle, had come to much the same conclusion. He was very fond of Bob, but two missed catches in one over was straining the bonds of human affection too far. There would have been serious trouble between David and Jonathan if either had persisted in dropping catches off the other's bowling. He writhed in bed as he remembered the second of the two chances which the wretched Bob had refused. The scene was indelibly printed on his mind. Chap had got a late cut which he fancied rather. With great guile he had fed this late cut. Sent down a couple which he put to the boundary. Then fired a third much faster and a bit shorter. Chap had a go at it, just as he had expected: and he felt that life was a good thing after all when the ball just touched the corner of the bat and flew into Bob's hands. And Bob dropped it!

The memory was too bitter. If he dwelt on it, he felt, he would get insomnia. So he turned to pleasanter reflections:

the yorker which had shattered the second-wicket man, and the slow head-ball which had led to a big hitter being caught on the boundary. Soothed by these memories, he fell asleep.

Next morning he found himself in a softened frame of mind. He thought of Bob's iniquities with sorrow rather than wrath. He felt towards him much as a father feels towards a prodigal son whom there is still a chance of reforming. He overtook Bob on his way to chapel.

Directness was always one of Burgess's leading qualities.

"Look here, Bob. About your fielding. It's simply awful."

Bob was all remorse.

"It's those beastly slip catches. I can't time them."

"That one yesterday was right into your hands. Both of them were."

"I know. I'm frightfully sorry."

"Well, but I mean, why *can't* you hold them? It's no good being a good bat—you're that all right—if you're going to give away runs in the field."

"Do you know, I believe I should do better in the deep. I could get time to watch them there. I wish you'd give me a shot in the deep—for the second."

"Second be blowed! I want your batting in the first. Do you think you'd really do better in the deep?"

"I'm almost certain I should. I'll practise like mad. Trevor'll hit me up catches. I hate the slips. I get in the dickens of a funk directly the bowler starts his run now. I know that if a catch does come, I shall miss it. I'm certain the deep would be much better."

"All right then. Try it."

The conversation turned to less pressing topics.

In the next two matches, accordingly, Bob figured on the boundary, where he had not much to do except throw the ball back to the bowler, and stop an occasional drive along the carpet. The beauty of fielding in the deep is that no unpleasant surprises can be sprung upon one. There is just that moment or two for collecting one's thoughts which makes the whole difference. Bob, as he stood regarding the game from afar, found his self-confidence returning slowly, drop by drop.

As for Mike, he played for the second, and hoped for the day.

His opportunity came at last. It will be remembered that on the morning after the Great Picnic the headmaster made an announcement in the Hall to the effect that, owing to an outbreak of chicken-pox in the town, all streets except the High Street would be out of bounds. This did not affect the bulk of the school, for most of the shops to which anyone ever thought of going were in the High Street. But there were certain inquiring minds who liked to ferret about in odd corners.

Among these was one Leather-Twigg, of Seymour's, better known in criminal circles as Shoeblossom.

Shoeblossom was a curious mixture of the Energetic Ragger and the Quiet Student. On a Monday evening you would hear a hideous uproar proceeding from Seymour's junior day-room; and, going down with a swagger-stick to investigate, you would find a tangled heap of squealing humanity on the floor, and at the bottom of the heap, squealing louder than any two others, would be Shoeblossom, his collar burst and blackened and his face apoplectically crimson. On the Tuesday afternoon, strolling in some shady corner of the grounds you would come upon him lying on his chest, deep in some work of fiction and resentful of interruption. On the Wednesday morning he would be in receipt of four hundred lines from his house-master for breaking three windows and a light bulb. Essentially a man of moods, Shoeblossom.

It happened about the date of the Geddington match that he took out from the school library a copy of *The Iron Pirate*, and for the next day or two he wandered about like a lost spirit trying to find a sequestered spot in which to read it. His inability to hit on such a spot was rendered more irritating by the fact that, to judge from the first few chapters (which he had managed to get through during prep one night under the eye of a short-sighted master), the book was obviously the last word in hot stuff. He tried the junior day-room, but people threw cushions at him. He tried out of doors, and a ball hit from a neighbouring net nearly scalped him. Anything in the nature of concentration became impossible in these circumstances.

Then he recollected that in a quiet backwater off the High Street there was a little confectioner's shop, where tea might be had at a reasonable sum, and, also, what was more important, peace.

He made his way there, and in the dingy back shop, all amongst the dust and bluebottles, settled down to a thoughtful perusal of chapter six.

Upstairs, at the same moment, the doctor was recommending that Master John George, the son of the house, be kept warm and out of draughts and not permitted to scratch himself, however necessary such an action might seem to him. In brief, he was attending J. G. for chickenpox.

Shoeblossom came away, entering the High Street furtively, lest Authority should see him out of bounds, and returned to the school, where he went about his lawful occasions as if there were no such thing as chicken-pox in the world.

But all the while the microbe was getting in some unostentatious but clever work. A week later Shoeblossom began to feel queer. He had occasional headaches, and found himself oppressed by a queer distaste for food. The professional advice of Dr. Oakes, the school doctor, was called for, and Shoeblossom took up his abode in the Infirmary, where he read *Punch*, sucked oranges, and thought of life.

Two days later Barry felt queer. He, too, disappeared from society.

Chicken-pox is no respecter of persons. The next victim was Marsh, of the first eleven. Marsh, who was top of the school averages. Where were his drives now, his late cuts that were wont to set the pavilion in a roar? Wrapped in a blanket, and looking like the spotted marvel of a travelling circus, he was driven across to the Infirmary in a car, and it became incumbent upon Burgess to select a substitute for him.

And so it came about that Mike soared once again into the ranks of the elect, and found his name down in the team to play against the Incogniti.

CHAPTER XVIII

BOB HAS NEWS TO IMPART

WRYKYN went down badly before the Incogs. It generally
happens at least once in a school cricket season
that the team collapses hopelessly, for no apparent reason.
Some schools do it in nearly every match, but Wrykyn so
far had been particularly fortunate this year. They had
only been beaten once, and that by a mere twenty-odd runs
in a hard-fought game. But on this particular day, against
a not overwhelmingly strong side, they failed miserably.
The weather may have had something to do with it, for
rain fell early in the morning, and the school, batting first
on the drying wicket, found themselves considerably
puzzled by a slow left-hander. Morris and Berridge left
with the score still short of ten, and after that the rout
began. Bob, going in fourth wicket, made a dozen, and
Mike kept his end up, and was not out eleven; but nobody
except Wyatt, who hit out at everything and knocked up
thirty before he was stumped, did anything to distinguish
himself. The total was a hundred and seven, and the
Incogniti, batting when the wicket was easier, doubled
this.

The general opinion of the school after this match was
that either Mike or Bob would have to stand down from
the team when it was definitely filled up, for Neville-Smith,
by showing up well with the ball against the Incogniti
when the others failed with the bat, made it practically
certain that he would get one of the two vacancies.

"If I do," he said to Wyatt, "there will be the biggest
bust-up of modern times at my place. My father is away

for a holiday in Norway, and I'm alone, bar the servants. And I can square them. Will you come?"

"Tea?"

"Tea!" said Neville-Smith scornfully.

"Well, what then?"

"Don't you ever have feeds in the dorms after lights-out in the houses?"

"Used to when I was a kid. Too old now. Have to look after my digestion. I remember, three years ago, when Wain's won the rugger cup, we got up and fed at about two in the morning. All sorts of luxuries. Sardines on sugar-biscuits. I've got the taste in my mouth still. Do you remember Macpherson? Left a couple of years ago. His food ran out, so he spread brown-boot polish on bread, and ate that. Got through a slice, too. Wonderful chap! But what about this thing of yours? What time's it going to be?"

"Eleven suit you?"

"All right."

"How about getting out?"

"I'll do it as quickly as the team did today. I can't say more than that."

"You were all right."

"I'm an exceptional sort of chap."

"What about the Jacksons?"

"It's going to be a close thing. If Bob's fielding were to improve suddenly, he would just do it. But young Mike's all over him as a bat. In a year or two that kid'll be a marvel. He's bound to get in next year, of course, so perhaps it would be better if Bob got the place as it's his last season. Still, one wants the best man, of course."

Mike avoided Bob as much as possible during this anxious period; and he privately thought it rather tactless of the latter when, meeting him one day outside Donaldson's, he insisted on his coming in and having some tea.

Mike shuffled uncomfortably as his brother filled the

kettle and lit the gas-ring. It required more tact than he had at his disposal to carry off a situation like this.

Bob, being older, was more at his ease. He got tea ready, making desultory conversation the while, as if there were no particular reason why either of them should feel uncomfortable in the other's presence. When he had finished, he poured Mike out a cup, passed him the bread, and sat down.

"Not seen much of each other lately, Mike, what?"

Mike murmured unintelligibly through a mouthful of bread-and-jam.

"It's no good pretending it isn't an awkward situation," continued Bob, "because it is. Beastly awkward."

"Awful bind, Father sending us to the same school."

"Oh, I don't know. We've all been at Wrykyn. Pity to spoil the record. It's your fault for being such a young Infant Prodigy, and mine for not being able to field like an ordinary human being."

"You get on much better in the deep."

"Bit better, yes. Liable at any moment to miss a sitter, though. Not that it matters much really whether I do now."

Mike stared.

"What! Why?"

"That's what I wanted to see you about. Has Burgess said anything to you yet?"

"No. Why? What about?"

"Well, I've a sort of idea our little race is over. I fancy you've won."

"I've not heard a word——"

"I have. I'll tell you what makes me think the thing's settled. I was in the pav just now, in the first room, trying to find a batting-glove I'd mislaid. There was a copy of the *Wrykynian* lying on the mantelpiece, and I picked it up and started reading it. So there wasn't any noise to show anybody outside that there was someone in the room. And then I heard Burgess and Spence jawing on the steps. They thought the place was empty, of course. I couldn't help hearing what they said. The pav's like a sounding-board. I heard every word. Spence said, 'Well, it's about as difficult a problem as any captain of cricket at Wrykyn has ever had to tackle.' I had a sort of idea that old Billy liked to boss things all on his own, but apparently he does consult Spence sometimes. After all, he's cricket-master, and that's what he's there for. Well, Billy said, 'I don't know what to do. What do you think, sir?' Spence said, 'Well, I'll give you my opinion, Burgess, but don't feel bound to act on it. I'm simply saying what I think.' 'Yes, sir,' said old Bill, doing a big Young Disciple with Wise Master act. '*I* think M.,' said Spence. 'Decidedly M. He's a shade better than R. now, and in a year or two, of course, there'll be no comparison.'"

"Oh, rot," muttered Mike, wiping the sweat off his forehead. This was one of the most harrowing interviews he had ever been through.

"Not at all. Billy agreed with him. 'That's just what I think, sir,' he said. 'It's rough on Bob, but still——' And then they walked down the steps. I waited a bit to give them a good start, and then sheered off myself. And so home."

Mike looked at the floor, and said nothing.

There was nothing much to *be* said.

"Well, what I wanted to see you about was this," resumed Bob. "I don't propose to kiss you or anything; but, on the other hand, don't let's go to the other extreme. I'm not saying that it isn't a bit of a brick just missing my cap like this, but it would have been just as bad for you if you'd been the one dropped. It's the fortune of war. I don't want you to go about feeling that you've blighted my life, and so on, and dashing up side-streets to avoid me because you think the sight of you will be painful. As it isn't me, I'm jolly glad it's you; and I shall cadge a seat in the pavilion from you when you're playing for England at the Oval. Congratulate you."

It was the custom at Wrykyn, when you congratulated a man on getting colours, to shake his hand. They shook hands.

"Thanks, awfully, Bob," said Mike. And after that there seemed to be nothing much to talk about. So Mike edged out of the room, and tore across to Wain's.

He was sorry for Bob, but he would not have been human (which he certainly was) if the triumph of having won through at last into the first eleven had not dwarfed commiseration. It had been his one ambition, and now he had achieved it.

The annoying part of the thing was that he had nobody to talk to about it. Until the news was official he could not mention it to the common herd. It wouldn't do. The only possible confidant was Wyatt. And Wyatt was at Bisley, shooting with the School Eight for the Ashburton. For bull's-eyes as well as cats came within Wyatt's range as a marksman. Cricket took up too much of his time for him to be captain of the Eight and the man chosen to shoot for the Spencer, as he would otherwise almost certainly have been; but, even though short of practice, he was well up in the team.

Until he returned, Mike could tell nobody. And by the time he returned the notice would probably be up in the Senior Block with the other cricket notices.

In this fermenting state Mike went into the house.

The list of the team to play for Wain's *v.* Seymour's on the following Monday was on the board. As he passed it, a few words scrawled in pencil at the bottom caught his eye.

"All the above will turn out for house-fielding at six-thirty tomorrow morning.—W. F.-S."

"Oh, dash it," said Mike, "what rot! Why on earth can't he leave us alone!"

For getting up an hour before his customary time for rising was not among Mike's favourite pastimes. Still, orders were orders, he felt. It would have to be done.

CHAPTER XIX

MIKE GOES TO SLEEP AGAIN

MIKE was a stout supporter of the view that sleep in large quantities is good for one. He belonged to the school of thought which holds that a man becomes plain and pasty if deprived of his full spell in bed. He aimed at the peach-bloom complexion.

To be routed out of bed a clear hour before the proper time, even on a summer morning, was not, therefore, a prospect that appealed to him.

When he woke it seemed even less attractive than it had done when he went to sleep. He had banged his head on the pillow six times over-night, and this silent alarm proved effective, as it always does. Reaching out a hand for his watch, he found that it was five minutes past six.

This was to the good. He could manage another quarter of an hour between the sheets. It would only take him ten minutes to wash and get into his flannels.

He took his quarter of an hour, and a little more. He woke from a sort of doze to find that it was twenty-five past.

Man's inability to get out of bed in the morning is a curious thing. One may reason with oneself clearly and forcibly without the slightest effect. One knows that delay means inconvenience. Perhaps it may spoil one's whole day. And one also knows that a single resolute heave will do the trick. But logic is of no use. One simply lies there.

Mike thought he would take another minute.

And during that minute there floated into his mind the

question: Who *was* Firby-Smith? That was the point. Who *was* he, after all?

This started quite a new train of thought. Previously Mike had firmly intended to get up—some time. Now he began to waver.

The more he considered the Gazeka's insignificance and futility and his own magnificence, the more outrageous did it seem that he should be dragged out of bed to please Firby-Smith's vapid mind. Here was he, about to receive his first eleven colours on this very day probably, being ordered about, inconvenienced—in short, put upon by a worm who had only just scraped into the third.

Was this right? he asked himself. Was this proper?

And the hands of the watch moved round to twenty to.

What was the matter with his fielding? *It* was all right. Make the rest of the team fag about, yes. But not a chap who, dash it all, had got his first *for* fielding!

It was with almost a feeling of self-righteousness that Mike turned over on his side and went to sleep again.

And outside in the cricket field, the massive mind of the Gazeka was filled with rage, as it was gradually borne in upon him that this was not a question of mere lateness—which, he felt, would be bad enough, for when he said six-thirty he meant six-thirty—but of actual desertion. It was time, he said to himself, that the foot of Authority was set firmly down, and the strong right hand of Justice allowed to put in some energetic work. His comments on the team's fielding that morning were bitter and sarcastic. His eyes gleamed behind their pince-nez.

The painful interview took place after breakfast. The head of the house dispatched his fag in search of Mike, and waited. He paced up and down the room like a hungry lion, adjusting his pince-nez (a thing, by the way, which lions seldom do) and behaving in other respects like a monarch of the desert. One would have felt, looking at him, that Mike, in coming to his den, was doing a deed which would make the achievement of Daniel seem in comparison like the tentative effort of some timid novice.

And certainly Mike was not without qualms as he knocked at the door, and went in in response to the hoarse roar from the other side of it.

Firby-Smith straightened his tie, and glared.

"Young Jackson," he said, "look here, I want to know what it all means, and jolly quick. You weren't at house-fielding this morning. Didn't you see the notice?"

Mike admitted that he had seen the notice.

"Then you frightful kid, what do you mean by it? What?"

Mike hesitated. Awfully embarrassing, this. His real reason for not turning up to house-fielding was that he considered himself above such things, and Firby-Smith a toothy weed. Could he give this excuse? He had not his Book of Etiquette by him at the moment, but he rather fancied not. There was no arguing against the fact that the head of the house *was* a toothy weed; but he felt a firm conviction that it would not be polite to say so.

Happy thought: over-slept himself.

He mentioned this.

"Over-slept yourself! You must jolly well not over-sleep yourself. What do you mean by over-sleeping yourself?"

Very trying this sort of thing.

"What time did you wake up?"

"Six," said Mike.

It was not according to his complicated, yet intelligible code of morality to tell lies to save himself. When others were concerned he could suppress the true and suggest the false with a face of brass.

"Six!"

"Five past."

"Why didn't you get up then?"

"I went to sleep again."

"Oh, you went to sleep again, did you? Well, just listen to me. I've had my eye on you for some time, and I've seen it coming on. You've got swelled head, young man. That's what you've got. Frightful swelled head. You think the place belongs to you."

"I don't," said Mike indignantly.

"Yes, you do," said the Gazeka shrilly. "You think the whole frightful place belongs to you. You go stalking about as if you'd bought it. Just because you've got your second, you think you can do what you like; turn up or not, as you please. It doesn't matter whether I'm only in the third and you're in the first. That's got nothing to do with it. The point is that you're one of the house team, and I'm captain of it, so you've jolly well got to turn out for fielding with the others when I think it necessary. See?"

Mike said nothing.

"Do—you—see, you frightful kid?"

Mike remained stonily silent. The rather large grain of truth in what Firby-Smith had said had gone home, as the unpleasant truth about ourselves is apt to do; and his feelings were hurt. He was determined not to give in and say that he saw even if the head of the house invoked all the majesty of the prefects' room to help him, as he had nearly done once before. He set his teeth, and stared at a photograph on the wall.

Firby-Smith's manner became ominously calm. He produced a swagger-stick from a corner.

"Do you see?" he asked again.

Mike's jaw set more tightly.

What one really wants here is a row of stars.

Mike was still full of his injuries when Wyatt came back. Wyatt was worn out, but cheerful. The school had finished sixth for the Ashburton, which was an improvement of eight places on their last year's form, and he himself had scored thirty at the two hundred and twenty-seven at the five hundred totals, which had put him in a very good humour with the world.

"Me ancient skill has not deserted me," he said, "that's the cats. The man who can wing a cat by moonlight can put a bullet where he likes on a target. I didn't hit the bull every time, but that was to give the other fellows a chance. My fatal modesty has always been a hindrance to me in life, and I suppose it always will be. Well, well! And what of the old homestead? Anything happened since I went away? Me old father, is he well? Has the lost will been discovered, or is there a mortgage on the family estates? By Jove, I'm thirsty, I wonder if the moke's gone to bed yet. I'll go down and look. A jug of water drawn from the well in the old courtyard where my ancestors have played as children for centuries back would just about save my life."

He left the dormitory, and Mike began to brood over his wrongs once more.

Wyatt came back, brandishing a jug of water and a glass.

"Oh, for a beaker full of the warm south, full of the true, the blushful Hippocrene! Have you ever tasted Hippocrene, young Jackson? Rather like ginger-beer, with a dash of raspberry-vinegar. Very heady. Failing that, water will do. A-ah!"

He put down the glass, and surveyed Mike, who had maintained a moody silence throughout this speech.

"What's your trouble?" he asked. "For pains in the back try Ju-jar. If it's a broken heart, Zam-buk's what you want. Who's been quarrelling with you?"

"It's only that ass Firby-Smith."

"Again! I never saw such chaps as you two. Always at it. What was the trouble this time? Call him a grinning ape again? Your passion for the truth'll be getting you into trouble one of these days."

"He said I stuck on side."

"Why?"

"I don't know."

"I mean, did he buttonhole you on your way to school, and say, 'Jackson, a word in your ear. You stick on side.' Or did he lead up to it in any way? Did he say, 'Talking of side, you stick it on.' What had you been doing to him?"

"It was the house-fielding."

"But you can't stick on side at house-fielding. I defy anyone to. It's too early in the morning."

"I didn't turn up."

"What! Why?"

"Oh, I don't know."

"No, but, look here, really. Did you simply cut it?"

"Yes."

Wyatt leaned on the end of Mike's bed, and, having observed its occupant thoughtfully for a moment, proceeded to speak wisdom for the good of his soul.

"I say, I don't want to jaw—I'm one of those quiet chaps with strong, silent natures; you may have noticed it— but I must put in a well-chosen word at this juncture. Don't pretend to be dropping off to sleep. Sit up and listen to what your kind old uncle's got to say to you about manners and deportment. Otherwise, blood as you are at cricket, you'll have a rotten time here. There are some things you simply can't do; and one of them is cutting a thing when you're put down for it. It doesn't matter who it is puts you down. If he's captain, you've got to obey him. That's discipline, that 'ere is. The speaker then paused, and took a sip of water from the carafe which stood at his elbow. Cheers from the audience, and a voice 'Hear! Hear!'"

Mike rolled over in bed and glared up at the orator. Most of his face was covered by the water-jug, but his eyes stared fixedly from above it. He winked in a friendly way, and, putting down the jug, drew a deep breath.

"Nothing like this old '87 water," he said. "Such body."

"I like you jawing about discipline," said Mike morosely.

"And why, my gentle che-ild, should I not talk about discipline?"

"Considering you break out of the house nearly every night."

"In passing, rather rum when you think that a burglar would get it hot for breaking in, while I get dropped on if I break out. Why should there be one law for the burglar

and one for me? But you were saying—just so. I thank
you. About my breaking out. When you're a white-
haired old man like me, young Jackson, you'll see that
there are two sorts of discipline at school. One you can
break if you feel like taking the risks; the other you mustn't
ever break. I don't know why, but it isn't done. Until
you learn that, you can never hope to become the Perfect
Wrykynian like," he concluded modestly, "me."

Mike made no reply. He would have perished rather
than admit it, but Wyatt's words had sunk in. That
moment marked a distinct epoch in his career. His feelings
were curiously mixed. He was still furious with Firby-
Smith, yet at the same time he could not help acknowledging
to himself that the latter had had the right on his side. He
saw and approved of Wyatt's point of view, which was the
more impressive to him from his knowledge of his friend's
contempt for, or, rather, cheerful disregard of, most forms
of law and order. If Wyatt, reckless though he was as
regarded written school rules, held so rigid a respect for
those that were unwritten, these last must be things which
could not be treated lightly. That night, for the first time
in his life, Mike went to sleep with a clear idea of what the
public school spirit, of which so much is talked and written,
really meant.

CHAPTER XX

THE TEAM IS FILLED UP

WHEN Burgess, at the end of the conversation in the pavilion with Mr. Spence which Bob Jackson had overheard, accompanied the cricket-master across the field to the boarding-houses, he had distinctly made up his mind to give Mike his first eleven colours next day. There was only one more match to be played before the school fixture-list was finished. That was the match with Ripton. Both at cricket and rugger Ripton was the school that mattered most. Wrykyn did not always win its other school matches; but it generally did. The public schools of England divide themselves naturally into little groups, as far as games are concerned. Harrow, Eton, and Winchester are one group: Westminster and Charterhouse another: Bedford, Tonbridge, Dulwich, Haileybury and St. Paul's are a third. In this way, Wrykyn, Ripton, Geddington, and Wilborough formed a group. There was no actual championship competition, but each played each, and by the end of the season it was easy to see which was entitled to first place. This nearly always lay between Ripton and Wrykyn. Sometimes an exceptional Geddington team would sweep the board, or Wrykyn, having beaten Ripton, would go down before Wilborough. But this did not happen often. Usually Wilborough and Geddington were left to scramble for the wooden spoon.

Secretaries of cricket at Ripton and Wrykyn always liked to arrange the date of the match towards the end of the term, so that they might take the field with representative and not experimental teams. By July the weeding-out process had generally finished. Besides which the members of the teams had had time to get into form.

At Wrykyn it was the custom to fill up the team, if possible, before the Ripton match. A player is likely to show better form if he has got his colours than if his fate depends on what he does in that particular match.

Burgess, accordingly, had resolved to fill up the first eleven just a week before Ripton visited Wrykyn. There were two vacancies. One gave him no trouble. Neville-Smith was not a great bowler, but he was steady, and he had done well in the earlier matches. He had fairly earned his place. But the choice between Bob and Mike had kept him awake into the small hours two nights in succession. Finally he had consulted Mr. Spence, and Mr. Spence had voted for Mike.

Burgess was glad the thing was settled. The temptation to allow sentiment to interfere with business might have become too strong if he had waited much longer. He knew that it would be a wrench definitely excluding Bob from the team, and he hated to have to do it. The more he thought of it, the sorrier he was for him. If he could have pleased himself, he would have kept Bob in. But, as the poet has it, "Pleasure is pleasure, and biz is biz, and kep' in a sepyrit jug." The first duty of a captain is to have no friends.

From small causes great events do spring. If Burgess had not picked up a particularly interesting novel after breakfast on the morning of Mike's interview with Firby-Smith in the study, the list would have gone up on the notice-board after prayers. As it was, engrossed in his book, he let the moments go by till the sound of the bell startled him into movement. And then there was only time to gather up his cap, and sprint. The paper on which he had intended to write the list and the pen he had laid out to write it with lay untouched on the table.

And, as it was not his habit to put up notices except

during the morning, he postponed the thing. He could write it after tea. After all, there was a week before the match.

When school was over, he went across to the Infirmary to inquire about Marsh. The report was more than favourable. Marsh had better not see anyone just yet, in case of accident, but he was certain to be out in time to play against Ripton.

"Dr. Oakes thinks he will be back in school on Tuesday."

"Grand!" said Burgess, feeling that life was good. To take the field against Ripton without Marsh would have been to court disaster. Marsh's fielding alone was worth the money. With him at short slip, Burgess felt safe when he bowled.

The uncomfortable burden of the knowledge that he was about temporarily to sour Bob Jackson's life ceased for the moment to trouble him. He crooned extracts from musical comedy as he walked towards the nets.

Recollection of Bob's hard case was brought to him by the sight of that about-to-be-soured sportsman tearing across the ground in the middle distance in an effort to get to a high catch which Trevor had hit up to him. It was a difficult catch, and Burgess waited to see if he would bring it off.

Bob got to it with one hand, and held it. His impetus carried him on almost to where Burgess was standing.

"Well held," said Burgess.

"Hullo," said Bob awkwardly. A gruesome thought had flashed across his mind that the captain might think that this gallery-work was an organized advertisement.

"I couldn't get both hands to it," he explained.

"You're hot stuff in the deep."

"Easy when you're only practising."

"I've just been to the Infirmary."

"Oh. How's Marsh?"

"They wouldn't let me see him, but it's all right. He'll be able to play on Saturday."

"Good," said Bob, hoping he had said it as if he meant it. It was decidedly a blow. He was glad for the sake of the school, of course, but one has one's personal ambitions. To the fact that Mike and not himself was the eleventh cap he had become partially resigned: but he had wanted rather badly to play against Ripton.

Burgess passed on, his mind full of Bob once more. What hard luck it was! There was he, dashing about in the sun to improve his fielding, and all the time the team was filled up. He felt as if he were playing some low trick on a pal.

Then the Jekyll and Hyde business completed itself. He suppressed his personal feelings, and became the cricket captain again.

It was the cricket captain who, towards the end of the evening, came upon Firby-Smith and Mike parting at the conclusion of a conversation. That it had not been a friendly conversation would have been evident to the most casual observer from the manner in which Mike stumped off, swinging his cricket-bag as if it were a weapon of offence. There are many kinds of walk. Mike's was the walk of the Overwrought Soul.

"What's up?" inquired Burgess.

"Young Jackson, do you mean? Oh, nothing. I was only telling him that there was going to be house-fielding tomorrow before breakfast."

"Didn't he like the idea?"

"He's jolly well got to like it," said the Gazeka, as who should say: "This way for Iron Wills." "The frightful kid cut it this morning. There'll be worse trouble if he does it again."

There was, it may be mentioned, not an ounce of malice in the head of Wain's house. That by telling the captain of cricket that Mike had shirked fielding-practice he might injure the latter's prospects of a first eleven cap simply did not occur to him. That Burgess would feel, on being told of Mike's slackness, much as a bishop might feel if he heard that a favourite curate had become a Mahometan or a

Mumbo-Jumboist, did not enter his mind. All he considered was that the story of his dealings with Mike showed him, Firby-Smith, in the favourable and dashing character of the fellow-who-will-stand-no-nonsense, a sort of Captain Kettle on dry land, in fact; and so he proceeded to tell it in detail.

Burgess parted with him with the firm conviction that Mike was a young slacker. Keenness in fielding was a fetish with him; and to cut practice struck him as a crime.

He felt that he had been deceived in Mike.

When, therefore, one takes into consideration his private bias in favour of Bob, and adds to it the reaction caused by this sudden unmasking of Mike, it is not surprising that the list Burgess made out that night before he went to bed differed in an important respect from the one he had intended to write before school.

Mike happened to be near the notice-board when he pinned it up. It was only the pleasure of seeing his name down in black and white that made him trouble to look at the list. Bob's news of the day before yesterday had made it clear how that list would run.

The crowd that collected the moment Burgess had walked off carried him right up to the board.

He looked at the paper.

"Hard luck!" said somebody.

Mike scarcely heard him.

He felt physically sick with the shock of the disappointment. For the initial before the name Jackson was R.

There was no possibility of mistake. Since writing was invented, there had never been an R that looked less like an M than the one on that list.

Bob had beaten him on the tape.

CHAPTER XXI

MARJORY THE FRANK

AT the door of the senior block Burgess, going out, met Bob coming in, hurrying, as he was rather late.

"Congratulate you, Bob," he said; and passed on.

Bob stared after him. As he stared Trevor came out of the block.

"Congratulate you, Bob."

"What's the matter now?"

"Haven't you seen?"

"Seen what?"

"Why the list. You've got your first."

"My—what? You're rotting."

"No, I'm not. Go and look."

The thing seemed incredible. Had he dreamed that conversation between Spence and Burgess on the pavilion steps? Had he mixed up the names? He was certain that he had heard Spence give his verdict for Mike, and Burgess agree with him.

Just then, Mike, feeling very ill, came down the steps. He caught sight of Bob and was passing with a feeble grin, when something told him that this was one of those occasions on which one has to show a Red Indian fortitude and stifle one's private feelings.

"Congratulate you, Bob," he said awkwardly.

"Thanks awfully," said Bob, with equal awkwardness. Trevor moved on, delicately. This was no place for him. Bob's face was looking like a stuffed frog's, which was Bob's way of trying to appear unconcerned and at his ease, while Mike seemed as if at any moment he might burst into tears. Spectators are not wanted at these awkward interviews.

There was a short silence.

"Jolly glad you've got it," said Mike.

"I believe there's a mistake. I swear I heard Burgess say to Spence——"

"He changed his mind probably. No reason why he shouldn't."

"Well, it's jolly rummy."

Bob endeavoured to find consolation.

"Anyhow, you'll have three years in the first. You're a cert for next year."

"Hope so," said Mike, with such manifest lack of enthusiasm that Bob abandoned this line of argument. When one has missed one's colours, next year seems a very, very long way off.

They moved slowly through the cloisters, neither speaking, and up the stairs that led to the Great Hall. Each was gratefully conscious of the fact that prayers would be beginning in another minute, putting an end to an uncomfortable situation.

"Heard from home lately?" inquired Mike.

Bob snatched gladly at the subject.

"Got a letter from Mother this morning. I showed you the last one, didn't I? I've only just had time to skim through this one, as the post was late, and I only got it just as I was going to dash across to school. Not much in it. Here it is, if you want to read it."

"Thanks. It'll be something to do during maths."

"Marjory wrote to me, too, for the first time in her life. Haven't had time to look at it yet."

"After you. Sure it isn't meant for me? She owes me a letter."

"No, it's for me all right. I'll give it you in the interval."

The arrival of the headmaster put an end to the conversation.

. . . . .

By a quarter to eleven Mike had begun to grow reconciled to his fate. The disappointment was still there, but it was lessened. These things are like kicks on the shin. A brief spell of agony, and then a dull pain of which we are not always conscious unless our attention is directed to it, and which in time disappears altogether. When the bell rang for the interval that morning, Mike was, as it were, sitting up and taking nourishment.

He was doing this in a literal as well as in a figurative sense when Bob entered the school shop.

Bob appeared curiously agitated. He looked round, and, seeing Mike, pushed his way towards him through the crowd. Most of those present congratulated him as he passed; and Mike noticed, with some surprise, that, in place of the blushful grin which custom demands from the man who is being congratulated on receipt of colours, there appeared on his face a worried, even an irritated look. He seemed to have something on his mind.

"Hullo," said Mike amiably. "Got that letter?"

"Yes. I'll show it you outside."

"Why not here?"

"Come on."

Mike resented the tone, but followed. Evidently something had happened to upset Bob seriously. As they went out on the gravel, somebody congratulated Bob again, and again Bob hardly seemed to appreciate it.

Bob led the way across the gravel and on to the first terrace. When they had left the crowd behind, he stopped.

"What's up?" asked Mike.

"I want you to read——"

"Jackson!"

They both turned. The headmaster was standing on the edge of the gravel.

Bob pushed the letter into Mike's hands.

"Read that," he said, and went up to the headmaster. Mike heard the words "English Essay," and, seeing that the conversation was apparently going to be one of some length, "capped" the headmaster and walked off. He was just going to read the letter when the bell rang. He put the missive in his pocket, and went to his form-room wondering what Marjory could have found to say to Bob to touch him on the raw to such an extent. She was a breezy correspondent, with a style of her own, but usually she entertained rather than upset people. No suspicion of the actual contents of the letter crossed his mind.

He read it during school, under the desk; and ceased to wonder. Bob had had cause to look worried. For the thousand and first time in her career of crime Marjory had been and done it! With a strong hand she had shaken the cat out of the bag, and exhibited it plainly to all whom it might concern.

There was a curious absence of construction about the letter. Most authors of sensational matter nurse their bomb-shell, lead up to it, and display it to the best advantage. Marjory dropped hers into the body of the letter, and let it take its chance with the other news-items.

"Dear Bob [the letter ran],

"I hope you are quite well. I am quite well. Phyllis has a cold. Ella cheeked Mademoiselle yesterday, and had to write out 'Little Girls must be polite and obedient' a hundred times in French. She was jolly sick about it. I told her it served her right. Joe made eighty-three against Lancashire. Reggie made a duck. Have you got your first? If you have, it will be all through Mike. Uncle John told Father that Mike pretended to hurt his wrist so that you could play instead of him for the school, and Father said it was very sporting of Mike but nobody must tell you because it wouldn't be fair if you got your first for you to know that you owed it to Mike and I wasn't supposed to hear but I did because I was in the room only they didn't know I was (we were playing hide-and-seek and I was hiding) so I'm writing to tell you,

"From your affectionate sister
"Marjory."

There followed a P.S.

"I'll tell you what you ought to do. I've been reading a jolly good book called 'The Boys of Dormitory Two,' and the hero's an awfully nice boy named Lionel Tremayne, and his friend Jack Langdale saves his life when a beast of a boatman who's really employed by Lionel's cousin who wants the money that Lionel's going to have when he grows up stuns him and leaves him on the beach to drown. Well, Lionel is going to play for the school against Loamshire, and it's *the* match of the season, but he goes to the headmaster and says he wants Jack to play instead of him. Why don't you do that?

"M.

"P. P. S.—This has been a frightful fag to write."

For the life of him Mike could not help giggling as he pictured what Bob's expression must have been when his brother read this document. But the humorous side of the thing did not appeal to him for long. What should he say to Bob? What would Bob say to him? Dash it all, it made him look such an awful *ass*! Anyhow, Bob couldn't do much. In fact he didn't see that he could do anything. The team was filled up, and Burgess was not likely to alter it. Besides, why should he alter it? Probably he would have given Bob his colours anyhow. Still, it was beastly awkward. Marjory meant well, but she had put her foot right in it. Girls oughtn't to meddle with these things. No girl ought to be taught to write till she came of age. And Uncle John had behaved in many respects like the Complete Rotter. If he was going to let out things like that, he might at least have whispered them, or looked behind the curtains to see that the place wasn't chock-full of female kids. Confound Uncle John!

Throughout the dinner-hour Mike kept out of Bob's way. But in a small community like a school it is impossible to avoid a man for ever. They met at the nets.

"Well?" said Bob.

"How do you mean?" said Mike.

"Did you read it?"

"Yes."

"Well, is it all rot, or did you——you know what I mean—— sham a crocked wrist?"

"Yes," said Mike, "I did."

Bob stared gloomily at his toes.

"I mean," he said at last, apparently putting the finishing touch to some train of thought, "I know I ought to be grateful, and all that. I suppose I am. I mean it was jolly good of you—— Dash it all," he broke off hotly, as if the putting his position into words had suddenly showed him how inglorious it was, "what did you want to do it *for*? What was the idea? What right have you got to go about playing Providence over me? Dash it all, it's like giving a fellow money without consulting him."

"I didn't think you'd ever know. You wouldn't have if only that ass Uncle John hadn't let it out."

"How did he get to know? Why did you tell him?"

"He got it out of me. I couldn't choke him off. He came down when you were away at Geddington, and would insist on having a look at my arm, and naturally he spotted right away there was nothing the matter with it. So it came out; that's how it was."

Bob scratched thoughtfully at the turf with a spike of his boot.

"Of course, it was awfully decent——"

Then again the monstrous nature of the affair came home to him.

"But what did you do it *for*? Why should you ruin your own chances to give me a look in?"

"Oh, I don't know. . . . You know, you did *me* a jolly good turn."

"I don't remember. When?"

"That Firby-Smith business."

"What about it?"

"Well, you got me out of a jolly bad hole."

"Oh, rot! And do you mean to tell me it was simply because of that——?"

Mike appeared to him in a totally new light. He stared

at him as if he were some strange creature hitherto unknown to the human race. Mike shuffled uneasily beneath the scrutiny.

"Anyhow, it's all over now," Mike said, "so I don't see what's the point of talking about it."

"I'm hanged if it is. You don't think I'm going to sit tight and take my first as if nothing had happened?"

"What can you do? The list's up. Are you going to the Old Man to ask him if I can play, like Lionel Tremayne?"

The hopelessness of the situation came over Bob like a wave. He looked helplessly at Mike.

"Besides," added Mike, "I shall get in next year all right. Half a second, I just want to speak to Wyatt about something."

He sidled off.

"Well, anyhow," said Bob to himself, "I must see Burgess about it."

CHAPTER XXII

WYATT IS REMINDED OF AN ENGAGEMENT

THERE are situations in life which are beyond one. The sensible man realizes this, and slides out of such situations, admitting himself beaten. Others try to grapple with them, but it never does any good. When affairs get into a real tangle, it is best to sit still and let them straighten themselves out. Or, if one does not do that, simply to think no more about them. This is Philosophy. The true philosopher is the man who says "All right," and goes to sleep in his arm-chair. One's attitude towards Life's Little Difficulties should be that of the gentleman in the fable, who sat down on an acorn one day, and happened to doze. The warmth of his body caused the acorn to germinate, and it grew so rapidly that, when he awoke, he found himself sitting in the fork of an oak, sixty feet from the ground. He thought he would go home, but, finding this impossible, he altered his plans. "Well, well," he said, "if I cannot compel circumstances to my will, I can at least adapt my will to circumstances. I decide to remain here." Which he did, and had a not unpleasant time. The oak lacked some of the comforts of home, but the air was splendid and the view excellent.

Today's Great Thought for Young Readers. Imitate this man.

Bob should have done so, but he had not the necessary amount of philosophy. He still clung to the idea that he and Burgess, in council, might find some way of making things right for everybody. Though, at the moment, he did not see how eleven caps were to be divided amongst twelve candidates in such a way that each should have one.

And Burgess, consulted on the point, confessed to the same inability to solve the problem. It took Bob at least a quarter of an hour to get the facts of the case into the captain's head, but at last Burgess grasped the idea of the thing. At which period he remarked that it was a rum business.

"Very rum," Bob agreed. "Still, what you say doesn't help us out much, seeing that the point is, what's to be done?"

"Why do anything?"

Burgess was a philosopher, and took the line of least resistance, like the man in the oak-tree.

"But I must do something," said Bob. "Can't you see how rotten it is for me?"

"I don't see why. It's not your fault. Very sporting of your brother and all that, of course, though I'm blowed if I'd have done it myself; but why should you do anything? You're all right. Your brother stood out of the team to let you in it, and here you *are*, in it. What's he got to grumble about?"

"He's not grumbling. It's me."

"What's the matter with you? Don't you want your first?"

"Not like this. Can't you see what a rotten position it is for me?"

"Don't you worry. You simply keep on saying you're all right. Besides, what do you want me to do? Alter the list?"

But for the thought of those unspeakable outsiders, Lionel Treymayne and his headmaster, Bob might have answered this question in the affirmative: but he had the public school boy's terror of seeming to pose or do anything theatrical. He would have done a good deal to put matters right, but he could *not* do the self-sacrificing young hero business. It would not be in the picture. These things, if they are to be done at school, have to be carried through stealthily, after Mike's fashion.

"I suppose you can't very well, now it's up. Tell you what, though, I don't see why I shouldn't stand out of the team for the Ripton match. I could easily fake up some excuse."

"I do. I don't know if it's occurred to you, but the idea is rather to win the Ripton match, if possible. So that I'm a lot keen on putting the best team into the field. Sorry if it upsets your arrangements in any way."

"You know perfectly well Mike's every bit as good as me."

"He isn't so keen."

"What do you mean?"

"Fielding. He's a young slacker."

When Burgess had once labelled a man as that, he did not readily let the idea out of his mind.

"Slacker? What rot! He's as keen as anything."

"Anyhow, his keenness isn't enough to make him turn out for house-fielding. If you really want to know, that's why you've got your first instead of him. You sweated away, and improved your fielding twenty per cent; and I happened to be talking to Firby-Smith and found that young Mike had been shirking his, so out he went. A bad field's bad enough, but a slack field wants skinning."

"Smith oughtn't to have told you."

"Well, he did tell me. So you see how it is. There won't be any changes from the team I've put up on the board."

"Oh, all right," said Bob. "I was afraid you mightn't be able to do anything. So long."

"Mind the step," said Burgess.

At about the time when this conversation was in progress, Wyatt, crossing the cricket field towards the school shop in search of something fizzy that might correct a burning thirst acquired at the nets, espied on the horizon a suit of cricket flannels surmounted by a huge, expansive grin. As the distance between them lessened, he discovered that inside the flannels was Neville-Smith's body and behind the grin the rest of Neville-Smith's face. Their visit to the nets not having coincided in point of time, as the Greek exercise books say, Wyatt had not seen his friend since the list of the team had been posted on the board, so he proceeded to congratulate him on his colours.

"Thanks," said Neville-Smith, with a brilliant display of front teeth.

"Feeling good?"

"Not the word for it. I feel like—I don't know what."

"I'll tell you what you look like, if that's any good to you. That slight smile of yours will meet behind, if you don't look out, and then the top of your head'll come off."

"I don't care. I've got my first, whatever happens. Little Willie's going to buy a nice new cap and a pretty striped jacket all for his own self! I say, thanks for reminding me. Not that you did, but supposing you had. At any rate, I remember what it was I wanted to say to you. You know what I was saying to you about the bust-up I meant to have at home in honour of my getting my first, if I did, which I have—well, anyhow it's tonight. You can roll up, can't you?"

"Delighted. Anything for a free feed in these hard times. What time did you say it was?"

"Eleven. Make it a bit earlier, if you like."

"No, eleven'll do me all right."

"How are you going to get out?"

"'Stone walls do not a prison make, nor iron bars a cage.' That's what the man said who wrote the libretto for the last set of Latin Verses we had to do. I shall manage it."

"They ought to allow you a latch-key."

"Yes, I've often thought of asking my father for one. Still, I get on very well. Who are coming besides me?"

"No boarders. They all funked it."

"The race is degenerating."

"Said it wasn't good enough."

"The school is going to the dogs. Who did you ask?"

"Clowes was one. Said he didn't want to miss his

beauty sleep. And Henfrey backed out because he thought the risk of being sacked wasn't good enough."

"That's an aspect of the thing that might occur to some people. I don't blame him—I might feel like that myself if I'd got another couple of years at school."

"But one or two day-boys are coming. Clephane is, for one. And Beverley. We shall have rather a rag. I'm going to get the things now."

"When I get to your place—I don't believe I know the way, now I come to think of it—what do I do? Ring the bell and send in my card? Or smash the nearest window and climb in?"

"Don't make too much row, for goodness' sake. All the servants'll have gone to bed. You'll see the window of my room. It's just above the porch. It'll be the only one lighted up. Heave a pebble at it, and I'll come down."

"So will the glass—with a run, I expect. Still, I'll try to do as little damage as possible. After all, I needn't throw a brick."

"You *will* turn up, won't you?"

"Nothing shall stop me."

"Good man."

As Wyatt was turning away, a sudden compunction seized upon Neville-Smith. He called him back.

"I say, you don't think it's too risky, do you? I mean, you always are breaking out at night, aren't you? I don't want to get you into a row."

"Oh, that's all right," said Wyatt. "Don't you worry about me. I should have gone out anyhow tonight."

CHAPTER XXIII

A SURPRISE FOR MR. APPLEBY

"You may not know it," said Wyatt to Mike in the dormitory that night, "but this is the maddest, merriest day of all the glad New Year."

Mike could not help thinking that for himself it was the very reverse, but he did not state his view of the case.

"What's up?" he asked.

"Neville-Smith's giving a meal at his place in honour of his getting his first. I understand the preparations are on a scale of the utmost magnificence. No expense has been spared. Ginger-beer will flow like water. The oldest cask of lemonade has been broached; and a sardine is roasting whole in the market-place."

"Are you going?"

"If I can tear myself away from your delightful society. The kick-off is fixed for eleven sharp. I am to stand underneath his window and heave bricks till something happens. I don't know if he keeps a dog. If so, I shall probably get bitten to the bone."

"When are you going to start?"

"About five minutes after Wain has been round the dormitories to see that all's well. That ought to be somewhere about half-past ten."

"Don't go getting caught."

"I shall do my little best not to be. Rather tricky work, though, getting back. I've got to climb garden walls, and I shall probably be so full of ginger-pop that you'll be able to hear it swishing about inside me. No catch steeple-chasing if you're like that. They've no thought for people's convenience here. Now at Bradford they've got studies on the ground floor, the windows looking out over the boundless prairie. No climbing or steeple-chasing needed at all. All you have to do is to open the window and step out. Still, we must make the best of things. Push us over a pinch of that tooth-powder of yours. I've used all mine."

Wyatt very seldom penetrated further than his own garden on the occasions when he roamed abroad at night. For cat-shooting the Wain spinneys were unsurpassed. There was one particular dustbin where one might be certain of flushing a covey any night; and the wall by the potting-shed was a feline club-house.

But when he did wish to get out into the open country he had a special route which he always took. He climbed down from the wall that ran beneath the dormitory window into the garden belonging to Mr. Appleby, the master who had the house next to Mr. Wain's. Crossing this, he climbed another wall, and dropped from it into a small lane, which ended in the main road leading to Wrykyn town.

This was the route which he took tonight. It was a glorious July night, and the scent of the flowers came to him with a curious distinctness as he let himself down from the dormitory window. At any other time he might have made a lengthy halt, and enjoyed the scents and small summer noises, but now he felt that it would be better not to delay. There was a full moon, and where he stood he could be seen distinctly from the windows of both houses. They were all dark, it is true, but on these occasions it was best to take no risks.

He dropped cautiously into Appleby's garden, ran lightly across it, and was in the lane within a minute.

There he paused, dusted his trousers, which had suffered on the two walls, and strolled meditatively in the direction of the town. Half-past ten had just chimed from the school clock. He was in plenty of time.

"What a night!" he said to himself, sniffing as he walked.

Now it happened that he was not alone in admiring the beauty of that particular night. At ten-fifteen it had struck Mr. Appleby, looking out of his study into the moonlit school grounds, that a pipe in the open would make an excellent break in his night's work. He had acquired a slight headache as the result of correcting a batch of examination papers, and he thought that an interval of an hour in the open air before approaching the half-dozen or so papers which still remained to be looked at might do him good. The window of his study was open, but the room had got hot and stuffy. Nothing like a little fresh air for putting him right.

For a few moments he debated the rival claims of a stroll in the cricket field and a seat in the garden. Then he decided on the latter. The little gate in the railings opposite his house might not be open, and it was a long way round to the main entrance. So he took a deck-chair which leaned against the wall, and let himself out of the back door.

He took up his position in the shadow of a fir-tree with his back to the house. From here he could see the long garden. He was fond of his garden, and spent what few moments he could spare from work and games pottering about it. He had his views as to what the ideal garden should be, and he hoped in time to tinker his own three acres up to the desired standard. At present there remained much to be done. Why not, for instance, take away those laurels at the end of the lawn, and have a flower-bed there instead? Laurels lasted all the year round, true, whereas flowers died and left an empty brown bed in the winter, but then laurels were nothing much to look at at any time, and a garden always had a beastly appearance in winter, whatever you did to it. Much better have flowers, and get a decent show for one's money in summer at any rate.

The problem of the bed at the end of the lawn occupied his complete attention for more than a quarter of an hour, at the end of which period he discovered that his pipe had gone out.

He was just feeling for his matches to relight it when Wyatt dropped with a slight thud into his favourite herbaceous border.

The surprise, and the agony of feeling that large shoes were trampling among his treasures kept him transfixed for just the length of time necessary for Wyatt to cross the garden and climb the opposite wall. As he dropped into the lane, Mr. Appleby recovered himself sufficiently to emit a sort of strangled croak, but the sound was too slight to reach Wyatt. That reveller was walking down the Wrykyn road before Mr. Appleby had left his chair.

It is an interesting point that it was the gardener rather than the schoolmaster in Mr. Appleby that first awoke to action. It was not the idea of a boy breaking out of his house at night that occurred to him first as particularly heinous; it was the fact that the boy had broken out *via* his herbaceous border. In four strides he was on the scene of the outrage, examining, on hands and knees, with the aid of the moonlight the extent of the damage done.

As far as he could see, it was not serious. By a happy accident Wyatt's shoes had gone home to right and left of precious plants but not on them. With a sigh of relief, Mr. Appleby smoothed over the cavities, and rose to his feet.

At this point it began to strike him that the episode affected him as a schoolmaster also.

In that startled moment when Wyatt had suddenly crossed his line of vision, he had recognized him. The moon had shone full on his face as he left the flower-bed. There was no doubt in his mind as to the identity of the intruder.

He paused, wondering how he should act. It was not an easy question. There was nothing of the spy about Mr. Appleby. He went his way openly, liked and respected by boys and masters. He always played the game. The difficulty here was to say exactly what the game was. Sentiment, of course, bade him forget the episode, treat it as if it had never happened. That was the simple way out of the difficulty. There was nothing unsporting about Mr. Appleby. He knew that there were times when a master might, without blame, close his eyes or look the other way. If he had met Wyatt out of bounds in the daytime, and it had been possible to convey the impression that he had not seen him, he would have done so. To be out of bounds is not a particularly deadly sin. A master must check it if it occurs too frequently, but he may use his discretion.

Breaking out at night, however, was a different thing, altogether. It was on another plane. There are times when a master must waive sentiment, and remember that he is in a position of trust, and owes a duty directly to his headmaster, and indirectly, through the headmaster, to the parents. He receives a salary for doing this duty, and, if he feels that sentiment is too strong for him, he should resign in favour of someone of tougher fibre.

This was the conclusion to which Mr. Appleby came over his relighted pipe. He could not let the matter rest where it was.

In ordinary circumstances it would have been his duty to report the affair to the headmaster but in the present case he thought that a slightly different course might be pursued. He would lay the whole thing before Mr. Wain, and leave him to deal with it as he thought best. It was one of the few cases where it was possible for an assistant master to fulfil his duty to a parent directly, instead of through the agency of the headmaster.

Knocking out the ashes of his pipe against a tree, he folded his deck-chair and went into the house. The examination papers were spread invitingly on the table, but they would have to wait. He turned out the light and walked round to Wain's.

There was a light in one of the ground-floor windows. He tapped on the window, and the sound of a chair being pushed back told him that he had been heard. The blind shot up, and he had a view of a room littered with books and papers, in the middle of which stood Mr. Wain, like a sea-beast among rocks.

Mr. Wain recognized his visitor and opened the window. Mr. Appleby could not help feeling how like Wain it was to work on a warm summer's night in a hermetically sealed room. There was always something queer and eccentric about Wyatt's step-father.

"Can I have a word with you, Wain?" he said.

"Appleby! Is there anything the matter? I was startled when you tapped. Exceedingly so."

"Sorry," said Mr. Appleby. "Wouldn't have disturbed you, only it's something important. I'll climb in through here, shall I? No need to unlock the door." And, greatly to Mr. Wain's surprise and rather to his disapproval, Mr. Appleby vaulted on to the window-sill, and squeezed through into the room.

CHAPTER XXIV

CAUGHT

"GOT some rather bad news for you, I'm afraid," began Mr. Appleby. "I'll smoke, if you don't mind. About Wyatt."

"James!"

"I was sitting in my garden a few minutes ago, having a pipe before finishing the rest of my papers, and Wyatt dropped from the wall on to my herbaceous border."

Mr. Appleby said this with a tinge of bitterness. The thing still rankled.

"James! In your garden! Impossible. Why, it is not a quarter of an hour since I left him in his dormitory."

"He's not there now."

"You astound me, Appleby. I am astonished."

"So was I."

"How is such a thing possible? His window is heavily barred."

"Bars can be removed."

"You must have been mistaken."

"Possibly," said Mr. Appleby, a little nettled. Gaping astonishment is always apt to be irritating. "Let's leave it at that, then. Sorry to have disturbed you."

"No, sit down, Appleby. Dear me, this is most extraordinary. Exceedingly so. You are certain it was James?"

"Perfectly. It's like daylight out of doors."

Mr. Wain drummed on the table with his fingers.

"What shall I do?"

Mr. Appleby offered no suggestion.

"I ought to report it to the headmaster. That is certainly the course I should pursue."

"I don't see why. It isn't like an ordinary case. You're the parent. You can deal with the thing directly. If you come to think of it, a headmaster's only a sort of middleman between boys and parents. He plays substitute for the parent in his absence. I don't see why you should drag in the Head at all here."

"There is certainly something in what you say," said Mr. Wain on reflection.

"A good deal. Tackle the boy when he comes in, and have it out with him. Remember that it must mean expulsion if you report him to the headmaster. He would have no choice. Everybody who has ever broken out of his house here and been caught has been expelled. I should strongly advise you to deal with the thing yourself."

"I will. Yes. You are quite right, Appleby. That is a very good idea of yours. You are not going?"

"Must. Got a pile of examination papers to look over. Good night."

"Good night."

Mr. Appleby made his way out of the window and through the gate into his own territory in a pensive frame of mind. He was wondering what would happen. He had taken the only possible course, and, if only Wain kept his head and did not let the matter get through officially to the headmaster, things might not be so bad for Wyatt after all. He hoped they would not. He liked Wyatt. It would be a thousand pities, he felt, if he were to be expelled. What would Wain do? What would *he* do in a similar case? It was difficult to say. Probably talk violently for as long as he could keep it up, and then consider the episode closed. He doubted whether Wain would have the common sense to do this. Altogether it was very painful and disturbing, and he was taking a rather gloomy view of the assistant master's lot as he sat down to finish off the rest of his examination papers. It was not all roses, the life of an assistant master at a public school. He had continually to be sinking his own individual sympathies in the claims of his duty. Mr. Appleby was the last man who would willingly have reported a boy for enjoying a midnight ramble. But he was the last man to shirk the duty of reporting him, merely because it was one decidedly not to his taste.

Mr. Wain sat on for some minutes after his companion had left, pondering over the news he had heard. Even now he clung to the idea that Appleby had made some extraordinary mistake. Gradually he began to convince himself of this. He had seen Wyatt actually in bed a quarter of an hour before—not asleep, it was true, but apparently on the verge of dropping off. And the bars across the window had looked so solid. . . . Could Appleby have been dreaming? Something of the kind might easily have happened. He had been working hard, and the night was warm. . . .

Then it occurred to him that he could easily prove or disprove the truth of his colleague's statement by going to the dormitory and seeing if Wyatt were there or not. If he had gone out, he would hardly have returned yet.

He took a torch and walked quietly upstairs.

Arrived at his step-son's dormitory, he turned the door-handle softly and went in. The light of the torch fell on both beds. Mike was there, asleep. He grunted, and turned over with his face to the wall as the light shone on his eyes. But the other bed was empty. Appleby had been right.

If further proof had been needed, one of the bars was missing from the window. The moon shone in through the empty space.

The house-master sat down quietly on the vacant bed. He switched the torch out, and waited there in the semi-darkness, thinking. For years he and Wyatt had lived in a state of armed neutrality, broken by various small encounters. Lately, by silent but mutual agreement, they had kept out of each other's way as much as possible, and it had become rare for the house-master to have to find fault officially with his step-son. But there had never been anything even remotely approaching friendship between them. Mr. Wain was not a man who inspired affection readily, least of all in those many years younger than himself. Nor did he easily grow fond of others. Wyatt he had regarded, from the moment when the threads of their lives became entangled, as a complete nuisance.

It was not, therefore, a sorrowful, so much as an exasperated, vigil that he kept in the dormitory. There was nothing of the sorrowing father about his frame of mind. He was the house-master about to deal with a mutineer, and nothing else.

This breaking-out, he reflected wrathfully, was the last straw. Wyatt's presence had been a nervous inconvenience to him for years. The time had come to put an end to it. It was with a comfortable feeling of magnanimity that he resolved not to report the breach of discipline to the headmaster. Wyatt should not be expelled. But he should leave, and that immediately. He would write to the bank before he went to bed, asking them to receive his step-son at once; and the letter should go by the first post next day. The discipline of the bank would be salutary and steadying. And—this was a particularly grateful reflection—a fortnight annually was the limit of the holiday allowed by the management to its junior employees.

Mr. Wain had arrived at this conclusion, and was beginning to feel a little cramped, when Mike Jackson suddenly sat up.

"Hullo!" said Mike.

"Go to sleep, Jackson, immediately," snapped the house-master.

Mike had often heard and read of people's hearts leaping to their mouths, but he had never before experienced that sensation of something hot and dry springing in the throat, which is what really happens to us on receipt of a bad shock. A sickening feeling that the game was up beyond all hope of salvation came to him. He lay down again without a word.

What a frightful thing to happen! How on earth had

this come about? What in the world had brought Wain to the dormitory at that hour? Poor old Wyatt! If it had upset *him* (Mike) to see the house-master in the room, what would be the effect of such a sight on Wyatt, returning from the revels at Neville-Smith's!

And what could he do? Nothing. There was literally no way out. His mind went back to the night when he had saved Wyatt by a brilliant *coup*. The most brilliant of *coups* could effect nothing now. Absolutely and entirely the game was up.

Every minute that passed seemed like an hour to Mike. Dead silence reigned in the dormitory, broken every now and then by the creak of the other bed, as the house-master shifted his position. Twelve boomed across the field from the school clock. Mike could not help thinking what a perfect night it must be for him to be able to hear the strokes so plainly. He strained his ears for any indication of Wyatt's approach, but could hear nothing. Then a very faint scraping noise broke the stillness, and presently the patch of moonlight on the floor was darkened.

At that moment Mr. Wain snapped on his flashlight.

The unexpected glare took Wyatt momentarily aback. Mike saw him start. Then he seemed to recover himself. In a calm and leisurely manner he climbed into the room.

"James!" said Mr. Wain. His voice sounded ominously hollow.

Wyatt dusted his knees, and rubbed his hands together.

"Hullo, is that you, Father!" he said pleasantly.

CHAPTER XXV

MARCHING ORDERS

A SILENCE followed. To Mike, lying in bed, holding his breath, it seemed a long silence. As a matter of fact it lasted for perhaps ten seconds. Then Mr. Wain spoke.

"You have been out, James?"

It is curious how in the more dramatic moments of life the inane remark is the first that comes to us.

"Yes, sir," said Wyatt.

"I am astonished. Exceedingly astonished."

"I got a bit of a start myself," said Wyatt.

"I shall talk to you in my study. Follow me there."

"Yes, sir."

He left the room, and Wyatt suddenly began to chuckle.

"I *say*, Wyatt!" said Mike, completely thrown off his balance by the events of the night.

Wyatt continued to giggle helplessly. He flung himself down on his bed, rolling with laughter. Mike began to get alarmed.

"It's all right," said Wyatt at last, speaking with difficulty. "But, I say, how long had he been sitting there?"

"It seemed hours. About an hour, I suppose, really."

"It's the funniest thing I've ever struck. Me sweating to get in quietly, and all the time him camping out on my bed!"

"But look here, what'll happen?"

Wyatt sat up.

"That reminds me. Suppose I'd better go down."

"What'll he do, do you think?"

"Ah, now, what!"

"But, I say, it's awful. What'll happen?"

"That's for him to decide. Speaking at a venture, I should say——"

"You don't think——?"

"The boot. The swift and sudden boot. I shall be sorry to part with you, but I'm afraid it's a case of 'Au revoir, my little Hyacinth.' We shall meet at Philippi. This is my Moscow. Tomorrow I shall go out into the night with one long, choking sob. Years hence a white-haired bank clerk will tap at your door when you're a prosperous professional cricketer with your photograph in *Wisden*. That'll be me. Well, I suppose I'd better go down. We'd better all get to bed *some* time tonight. Don't go to sleep."

"Not likely."

"I'll tell you all the latest news when I come back. Where are me slippers? Ha, 'tis well! Lead on, then, minions. I follow."

In the study Mr. Wain was fumbling restlessly with his papers when Wyatt appeared.

"Sit down, James," he said.

Wyatt sat down. One of his slippers fell off with a clatter. Mr. Wain jumped nervously.

"Only my slipper," exclaimed Wyatt. "It slipped."

Mr. Wain took up a pen, and began to tap the table.

"Well, James?"

Wyatt said nothing.

"I should be glad to hear your explanation of this disgraceful matter."

"The fact is——" said Wyatt.

"Well?"

"I haven't one, sir."

"What were you doing out of your dormitory, out of the house, at that hour?"

"I went for a walk, sir."

"And, may I inquire, are you in the habit of violating

the strictest school rules by absenting yourself from the house during the night?"

"Yes, sir."

"What?"

"Yes, sir."

"This is an exceedingly serious matter."

Wyatt nodded agreement with this view.

"Exceedingly."

The pen rose and fell with the rapidity of the cylinder of a motor-car. Wyatt, watching it, became suddenly aware that the thing was hypnotizing him. In a minute or two he would be asleep.

"I wish you wouldn't do that, Father. Tap like that, I mean. It's sending me to sleep."

"James!"

"It's like a woodpecker."

"Studied impertinence——"

"I'm very sorry. Only it *was* sending me off."

Mr. Wain suspended tapping operations, and resumed the thread of his discourse.

"I am sorry, exceedingly, to see this attitude in you, James. It is not fitting. It is in keeping with your behaviour throughout. Your conduct has been lax and reckless in the extreme. It is possible that you imagine that the peculiar circumstances of our relationship secure you from the penalties to which the ordinary boy——"

"No, sir."

"I need hardly say," continued Mr. Wain, ignoring the interruption, "that I shall treat you exactly as I should treat any other member of my house whom I had detected in the same misdemeanour."

"Of course," said Wyatt, approvingly.

"I must ask you not to interrupt me when I am speaking to you, James. I say that your punishment will be no whit less severe than would be that of any other boy. You have repeatedly proved yourself lacking in ballast and a respect for discipline in smaller ways, but this is a far more serious matter. Exceedingly so. It is impossible for me to overlook it, even were I disposed to do so. You are aware of the penalty for such an action as yours?"

"The sack," said Wyatt laconically.

"It is expulsion. You must leave the school. At once."

Wyatt nodded.

"As you know, I have already secured a nomination for you in the London and Oriental Bank. I shall write to-morrow to the manager asking him to receive you at once——"

"After all, they only gain an extra fortnight of me."

"You will leave directly I receive his letter. I shall arrange with the headmaster that you are withdrawn privately——"

"*Not* the sack?"

"Withdrawn privately. You will not go to school to-morrow. Do you understand? That is all. Have you anything to say?"

Wyatt reflected.

"No, I don't think——"

His eye fell on a tray bearing a decanter and a syphon.

"Oh, yes," he said. "Can't I mix you a whisky-and-soda, Father, before I go off to bed?"

"Well?" said Mike.

Wyatt kicked off his slippers, and began to undress.

"What happened?"

"We chatted."

"Has he let you off?"

"Like a gun. I shoot off almost immediately. To-morrow I take a well-earned rest away from school, and the day after I become the gay young bank clerk, all amongst the ink and ledgers."

Mike was miserably silent.

"Buck up," said Wyatt cheerfully. "It would have happened anyhow in another fortnight. So why worry?"

Mike was still silent. The reflection was doubtless philosophic, but it failed to comfort him.

CHAPTER XXVI

THE AFTERMATH

BAD news spreads quickly. By the quarter to eleven interval next day the facts concerning Wyatt and Mr. Wain were public property. Mike, as an actual spectator of the drama, was in great request as an informant. As he told the story to a group of sympathizers outside the school shop, Burgess came up, his eyes rolling in a fine frenzy.

"Anybody seen young—oh, here you are. What's all this about Jimmy Wyatt? They're saying he's been sacked, or some rot."

"So he has—at least, he's got to leave."

"What? When?"

"He's left already. He isn't coming to school again."

Burgess' first thought, as befitted a good cricket captain, was for his team.

"And the Ripton match on Saturday!"

Nobody seemed to have anything except silent sympathy at his command.

"Dash the man! Silly ass! What did he want to do it for! Poor old Jimmy, though!" he added after a pause. "What bad luck for him!"

"Beastly," agreed Mike.

"All the same," continued Burgess, with a return to the austere manner of the captain of cricket, "he might have chucked playing the goat till after the Ripton match. Look here, young Jackson, you'll turn out for fielding with the first this afternoon. You'll play on Saturday."

"All right," said Mike, without enthusiasm. The Wyatt disaster was too recent for him to feel much pleasure at playing against Ripton *vice* his friend, withdrawn.

Bob was the next to interview him. They met in the cloisters.

"Hullo, Mike!" said Bob. "I say, what's all this about Wyatt?"

"Wain caught him getting back into the dorm last night after Neville-Smith's, and he's taken him away from the school."

"What's he going to do? Going into that bank straight away?"

"Yes. You know, that's the part he hates most. He'd have been leaving anyhow in a fortnight, you see; only it's awful rot for a chap like Wyatt to have to go and froust in a bank for the rest of his life."

"He'll find it rather a change, I expect. I suppose you won't be seeing him before he goes?"

"I shouldn't think so. Not unless he comes to the dorm. during the night. He's sleeping over in Wain's part of the house, but I shouldn't be surprised if he nipped out after Wain has gone to bed. Hope he does, anyway."

"I should like to say good-bye. But I don't suppose it'll be possible."

They separated in the direction of their respective form-rooms. Mike felt bitter and disappointed at the way the news had been received. Wyatt was his best friend, his pal; and it offended him that the school should take the tidings of his departure as they had done. Most of them who had come to him for information had expressed a sort of sympathy with the absent hero of his story, but the chief sensation seemed to be one of pleasurable excitement at the fact that something big had happened to break the monotony of school routine. They treated the thing much as they would have treated the announcement that a record score had been made in first-class cricket. The school was not so much regretful as comfortably thrilled. And Burgess had actually cursed before sympathizing. Mike felt resentful towards Burgess. As a matter of fact, the cricket captain wrote a letter to Wyatt during preparation that night which would have satisfied even Mike's sense of what was fit. But Mike had no opportunity of learning this.

There was, however, one exception to the general rule, one member of the school who did not treat the episode as if it were merely an interesting and impersonal item of sensational news. Neville-Smith heard of what had happaned towards the end of the interval, and rushed off instantly in search of Mike. He was too late to catch him before he went to his form-room, so he waited for him at half-past twelve, when the bell rang for the end of morning school.

"I say, Jackson, is this true about old Wyatt?"

Mike nodded.

"What happened?"

Mike related the story for the sixteenth time. It was a melancholy pleasure to have found a listener who heard the tale in the right spirit. There was no doubt about Neville-Smith's interest and sympathy. He was silent for a moment after Mike had finished.

"It was all my fault," he said at length. "If it hadn't been for me, this wouldn't have happened. What a fool I was to ask him to my place! I might have known he would be caught."

"Oh, I don't know," said Mike.

"It was absolutely my fault."

Mike was not equal to the task of soothing Neville-Smith's wounded conscience. He did not attempt it. They walked on without further conversation till they reached Wain's gate, where Mike left him. Neville-Smith proceeded on his way, plunged in meditation.

The result of which meditation was that Burgess got a second shock before the day was out. Bob, going over to the nets rather late in the afternoon, came upon the captain of cricket standing apart from his fellow men with an expression on his face that spoke of mental upheavals on a vast scale.

"What's up?" asked Bob.

"Nothing much," said Burgess, with a forced and grisly calm. "Only that, as far as I can see, we shall play Ripton on Saturday with a sort of second eleven. You don't happen to have got sacked or anything, by the way, do you?"

"What's happened now?"

"Neville-Smith. In extra on Saturday. That's all. Only our first- and second-change bowlers out of the team for the Ripton match in one day. I suppose by tomorrow half the others'll have gone, and we shall take the field on Saturday with a scratch side of kids from the Junior School."

"Neville-Smith! Why, what's he been doing?"

"Apparently he gave a sort of supper to celebrate his getting his first, and it was while coming back from that that Wyatt got collared. Well, I'm blowed if Neville-Smith doesn't toddle off to the Old Man after school today and tell him the whole yarn! Said it was all his fault. What rot! Sort of thing that might have happened to anyone. If Wyatt hadn't gone to him, he'd probably have gone out somewhere else."

"And the Old Man shoved him in extra?"

"Next two Saturdays."

"Are Ripton strong this year?" asked Bob, for lack of anything better to say.

"Very, from all accounts. They whacked the M.C.C. Jolly hot team of M.C.C. too. Stronger than the one we drew with."

"Oh, well, you never know what's going to happen at cricket. I may hold a catch for a change."

Burgess grunted.

Bob went on his way to the nets. Mike was just putting on his pads.

"I say, Mike," said Bob. "I wanted to see you. It's about Wyatt. I've thought of something."

"What's that?"

"A way of getting him out of that bank. If it comes off, that's to say."

"By Jove, he'd jump at anything. What's the idea?"

"Why shouldn't he get a job of sorts out in the Argentine? There ought to be heaps of sound jobs going there for a chap like Wyatt. He's a jolly good shot, to start with. I shouldn't wonder if it wasn't rather a score to be able to shoot out there. And he can ride, I know."

"By Jove, I'll write to father tonight. He must be able to work it, I should think. He never chucked the show altogether, did he?"

Mike, as most other boys of his age would have been, was profoundly ignorant as to the details by which his father's money had been, or was being, made. He only knew vaguely that the source of revenue had something to do with the Argentine. His brother Joe had been born in Buenos Aires; and once, three years ago, his father had gone over there for a visit, presumably on business. All these things seemed to show that Mr. Jackson senior was a useful man to have about if you wanted a job in that Eldorado, the Argentine Republic.

As a matter of fact, Mike's father owned vast tracts of land up country, where countless sheep lived and had their being. He had long retired from active superintendence of his estate. Like Mr. Spenlow, he had a partner, a stout fellow with the work-taint highly developed, who asked nothing better than to be left in charge. So Mr. Jackson had returned to the home of his fathers, glad to be there again. But he still had a decided voice in the ordering of affairs on the ranches, and Mike was going to the fountain-head of things when he wrote to his father that night, putting forward Wyatt's claims to attention and ability to perform any sort of job with which he might be presented.

The reflection that he had done all that could be done tended to console him for the non-appearance of Wyatt either that night or next morning—a non-appearance which was due to the simple fact that he passed that night in a bed in Mr. Wain's dressing-room, the door of which that cautious pedagogue, who believed in taking no chances, locked from the outside on retiring to rest.

CHAPTER XXVII

THE RIPTON MATCH

MIKE got an answer from his father on the morning of the Ripton match. A letter from Wyatt also lay on his plate when he came down to breakfast.

Mr. Jackson's letter was short, but to the point. He said he would go and see Wyatt early in the next week. He added that being expelled from a public school was not the only qualification for success as a sheep-farmer, but that, if Mike's friend added to this a general intelligence and amiability, and a skill for picking off cats with an air-pistol and bull's-eyes with a Lee-Enfield, there was no reason why something should not be done for him. In any case he would buy him a lunch, so that Wyatt would extract at least some profit from his visit. He said that he hoped something could be managed. It was a pity that a boy accustomd to shoot cats should be condemned for the rest of his life to shoot nothing more exciting than his cuffs.

Wyatt's letter was longer. It might have been published under the title "My First Day in a Bank, by a Beginner." His advent had apparently caused little sensation. He had first had a brief conversation with the manager, which had run as follows:

"Mr. Wyatt?"

"Yes, sir."

"H'm. . . . Sportsman?"

"Yes, sir."

"Cricketer?"

"Yes, sir."

"Play rugger?"

"Yes, sir."

"H'm. . . . Racquets?"

"Yes, sir."

"Everything?"

"Yes, sir."

"H'm. . . , Well, you won't get any more of it now."

After which a Mr. Blenkinsop had led him up to a vast ledger, in which he was to inscribe the addresses of all out-going letters. These letters he would then stamp, and subsequently take in bundles to the post office. Once a week he would be required to buy stamps. "If I were one of those Napoleons of Finance," wrote Wyatt, "I should cook the accounts, I suppose, and embezzle stamps to an incredible amount. But it doesn't seem in my line. I'm afraid I wasn't cut out for a business career. Still, I have stamped this letter at the expense of the office, and entered it up under the heading 'Sundries,' which is a sort of start. Look out for an article in the *Wrykynian,* 'Hints for Young Criminals, by J. Wyatt, champion catch - as - catch - can stamp-stealer of the British Isles.' So long. I suppose you are playing against Ripton, now that the world of commerce has found that it can't get on without me. Mind you make a century, and then perhaps Burgess'll give you your first after all. There were twelve colours given three years ago, because one chap left at half-term and the man who played instead of him came off against Ripton."

This had occurred to Mike independently. The Ripton match was a special event, and the man who performed any outstanding feat against that school was treated as a sort of Horatius. Honours were heaped upon him. If he could only make a century! Or even fifty. Even twenty, if it got the school out of a tight place. He was as nervous on the Saturday morning as he had been on the morning of the M.C.C. match. It was Victory or Westminster Abbey now. To do only averagely well, to be among the ruck, would be as useless as not playing at all, as far as his chance of his first was concerned.

It was evident to those who woke early on the Saturday morning that this Ripton match was not likely to end in a draw. During the Friday rain had fallen almost incessantly in a steady drizzle. It had stopped late at night; and at six in the morning there was every prospect of another hot day. There was that feeling in the air which shows that the sun is trying to get through the clouds. The sky was a dull grey at breakfast-time, except where a flush of deeper colour gave a hint of the sun. It was a day on which to win the toss, and go in first. At eleven-thirty, when the match was timed to begin, the wicket would be too wet to be difficult. Runs would come easily till the sun came out and began to dry the ground. When that happened there would be trouble for the side that was batting.

Burgess, inspecting the wicket with Mr. Spence during the quarter to eleven interval, was not slow to recognize this fact.

"I should win the toss today, if I were you, Burgess," said Mr. Spence.

"Just what I was thinking, sir."

"That wicket's going to get nasty after lunch, if the sun comes out. A regular Laker wicket it's going to be."

"I wish we *had* Laker," said Burgess. "Or even Wyatt. It would just suit him, this."

Mr. Spence, as a member of the staff, was not going to be drawn into discussing Wyatt and his premature departure, so he diverted the conversation on to the subject of the general aspect of the school's attack.

"Who will go on first with you, Burgess?"

"Who do you think, sir? Ellerby? It might be his wicket."

Ellerby bowled medium inclining to slow. On a pitch that suited him he was apt to turn from leg and get people out caught at the wicket or short slip.

"Certainly, Ellerby. This end, I think. The other's yours, though I'm afraid you'll have a poor time bowling fast today. Even with plenty of sawdust I doubt if it will be possible to get a decent foothold till after lunch."

"I must win the toss," said Burgess. "It's a nuisance too, about our batting. Marsh will probably be dead out of form after being in the Infirmary so long. If he'd had a chance of getting a bit of practice yesterday, it might have been all right."

"That rain will have a lot to answer for if we lose. On a dry, hard wicket I'm certain we should beat them four times out of six. I was talking to a man who played against them for the Nomads. He said that on a true wicket there was not a great deal of sting in their bowling, but that they've got a slow leg-break man who might be dangerous on a day like this. A boy called de Freece. I don't know of him. He wasn't in the team last year."

"I know the chap. He played wing-three for them at rugger against us this year on their ground. He was crocked when they came here. He's a pretty useful chap all round, I believe. Plays racquets for them too."

"Well, my friend said he had one very dangerous ball, of the chinaman type. Looks as if it were going away, and comes in instead."

"I don't think a lot of that," said Burgess ruefully. "One consolation is, though, that that sort of ball is easier to watch on a slow wicket. I must tell the fellows to look out for it."

"I should. And, above all, win the toss."

Burgess and Maclaine, the Ripton captain, were old acquaintances. They had been at the same preparatory school, and they had played against one another at rugger and cricket for two years now.

"We'll go in first, Mac," said Burgess, as they met on the pavilion steps after they had changed.

"It's awfully good of you to suggest it," said Maclaine, "but I think we'll toss. It's a hobby of mine. You call."

"Heads."

"Tails it is. I ought to have warned you that you hadn't a chance. I've lost the toss five times running, so I was bound to win today."

"You'll put us in, I suppose?"

"Yes—after us."

"Oh, well, we shan't have long to wait for our knock, that's a comfort. Buck up and send someone in, and let's get at you."

And Burgess went off to tell the groundsman to have plenty of sawdust ready, as he would want the field paved with it.

The policy of the Ripton team was obvious from the first over. They meant to force the game. Already the sun was beginning to peep through the haze. For about an hour run-getting ought to be a tolerably simple process; but after that hour singles would be as valuable as threes and boundaries an almost unheard-of luxury.

So Ripton went in to hit.

The policy proved successful for a time, as it generally does. Burgess, who relied on a run that was a series of tiger-like leaps culminating in a spring that suggested that he meant to lower the long jump record, found himself badly handicapped by the state of the ground. In spite of frequent libations of sawdust, he was compelled to tread cautiously, and this robbed his bowling of much of its pace. The score mounted rapidly. Twenty came in ten minutes. At thirty-five the first wicket fell, run out.

At sixty, Ellerby, who had found the pitch too soft for him and had been expensive, gave place to Grant. Grant bowled what were supposed to be slow leg-breaks, but which did not always break. The change worked. Maclaine, after hitting the first two balls to the boundary, skied the third to Bob Jackson in the deep, and Bob, for whom constant practice had robbed this sort of catch of its terrors, held it.

A yorker from Burgess disposed of the next man before he could settle down; but the score, seventy-four for three wickets, was large enough in view of the fact that the pitch was already becoming more difficult, and was certain to get worse, to make Ripton feel that the advantage was with them. Another hour of play remained before lunch. The deterioration of the wicket would be slow during that period. The sun, which was now shining brightly, would put in its deadliest work from two o'clock onwards. Maclaine's instructions to his men were to go on hitting.

A too liberal interpretation of the meaning of the verb "to hit" led to the departure of two more Riptonians in the course of the next two overs. There is a certain type of school batsman who considers that to force the game means to swipe blindly at every ball on the chance of taking it half-volley. This policy sometimes leads to a boundary or two, as it did on this occasion, but it means that wickets will fall, as also happened now. Seventy-four for three became eighty-six for five. Burgess began to look happier.

His contentment increased when he got the next man leg-before-wicket with the total unaltered. At this rate Ripton would be out before lunch for under a hundred.

But the rot stopped with the fall of that wicket. Dashing tactics were laid aside. The pitch had begun to play tricks, and the pair now in settled down to watch the ball. They plodded on, scoring slowly and jerkily till the hands of the clock stood at half-past one. Then Ellerby, who had gone on again instead of Grant, beat the less steady of the pair with a ball that pitched on the middle stump and shot into the base of the off. A hundred and twenty had gone up on the board at the beginning of the over.

That period which is always so dangerous, when the wicket is bad, the ten minutes before lunch, proved fatal to two more of the enemy. The last man had just gone to the wicket, with the score at a hundred and thirty-one, when a quarter to two arrived, and with it the luncheon interval.

So far it was anybody's game.

CHAPTER XXVIII

MIKE WINS HOME

THE Ripton last-wicket man was de Freece, the slow bowler. He was apparently a young gentleman wholly free from the curse of nervousness. He wore a cheerful smile as he took guard before receiving the first ball after lunch, and Wrykyn had plenty of opportunity of seeing that that was his normal expression when at the wickets. There is often a certain looseness about the attack after lunch, and the bowler of googlies took advantage of it now. He seemed to be a batsman with only one hit; but he had also a very accurate eye, and his one hit, a semi-circular stroke, which suggested the golf links rather than the cricket field, came off with distressing frequency. He mowed Burgess's first ball to the square-leg boundary, missed his second, and snicked the third for three over long-slip's head. The other batsman played out the over, and de Freece proceeded to treat Ellerby's bowling with equal familiarity. The scoring-board showed an increase of twenty as the result of three overs. Every run was invaluable now, and the Ripton contingent made the pavilion re-echo as a fluky shot over mid-on's head sent up the hundred and fifty.

There are few things more exasperating to the fielding side than a last-wicket stand. It resembles in its effect the dragging-out of a book or play after the *dénouement* has been reached. At the fall of the ninth wicket the fieldsmen nearly always look on their outing as finished. Just a ball or two to the last man, and it will be their turn to bat. If the last man insists on keeping them out in the field, they resent it.

What made it especially irritating now was the knowledge that a straight yorker would solve the whole thing. But when Burgess bowled a yorker, it was not straight. And when he bowled a straight ball, it was not a yorker. A four and a three to de Freece, and a four bye sent up a hundred and sixty.

It was beginning to look as if this might go on for ever, when Ellerby, who had been missing the stumps by fractions of an inch for the last ten minutes, did what Burgess had failed to do. He bowled a straight, medium-paced yorker, and de Freece, swiping at it with a bright smile, found his leg-stump knocked back. He had made twenty-eight. His record score, he explained to Mike, as they walked to the pavilion, for this or any ground.

The Ripton total was a hundred and sixty-six.

With the ground in its usual true, hard condition, Wrykyn would have gone in against a score of a hundred and sixty-six with the cheery intention of knocking off the runs for the loss of two or three wickets. It would have been a gentle canter for them.

But ordinary standards would not apply here. On a good wicket Wrykyn that season were a two hundred and fifty to three hundred side. On a bad wicket—well, they had met the Incogniti on a bad wicket, and their total—with Wyatt playing and making top score—had worked out at a hundred and seven.

A grim determination to do their best, rather than confidence that their best, when done, would be anything record-breaking, was the spirit which animated the team when they opened their innings.

And in five minutes this had changed to a dull gloom.

The tragedy started with the very first ball. It hardly seemed that the innings had begun, when Morris was seen to leave the crease, and make for the pavilion.

"It's that googly man," said Burgess blankly.

"What's happened?" shouted a voice from the interior of the first-eleven room.

"Morris is out!"

"Good gracious! How?" asked Ellerby, emerging from the room with one pad on his leg and the other in his hand.

"L.b.w. First ball."

My aunt! Who's in next? Not me?"

"No. Berridge. For goodness' sake, Berry, stick a bat in the way, and not your legs. Watch that de Freece man like a hawk. He breaks like sin all over the shop. Hullo, Morris! Bad luck! Were you out, do you think?" A batsman who has been given l.b.w. is always asked this question on his return to the pavilion, and he answers it in nine cases out of ten in the negative. Morris was the tenth case. He thought it was all right, he said.

"Thought the thing was going to break, but it didn't."

"Hear that, Berry? He doesn't always break. You must look out for that," said Burgess helpfully. Morris sat down and began to take off his pads.

"That chap'll have Berry, if he doesn't look out," he said.

But Berridge survived the ordeal. He turned his first ball to leg for a single.

This brought Marsh to the batting end; and the second tragedy occurred.

It was evident from the way he shaped that Marsh was short of practice. His visit to the Infirmary had taken the edge off his batting. He scratched awkwardly at three balls without hitting them. The last of the over had him in two minds. He started to play forward, changed his stroke suddenly and tried to step back, and the next moment the bails had shot up like the *débris* of a small explosion, and the wicket-keeper was clapping his gloved hands gently and slowly in the introspective, dreamy way wicket-keepers have on these occasions.

A silence that could be felt brooded over the pavilion.

The voice of the scorer, addressing from his little wooden hut the melancholy youth who was working the telegraph-board, broke it.

"One for two.   Last man duck."

Ellerby echoed the remark.   He got up, and took off his blazer.

"This is all right," he said, "isn't it!   I wonder if the man at the other end is a sort of young Tattersall too!"

Fortunately he was not.   The star of the Ripton attack was evidently de Freece.   The bowler at the other end looked fairly plain.   He sent them down medium-pace, and on a good wicket would probably have been simple. But today there was danger in the most guileless-looking deliveries.

Berridge relieved the tension a little by playing safely through the over, and scoring a couple of two's off it. And when Ellerby not only survived the destructive de Freece's second over, but actually lifted a loose ball on to the roof of the scoring-hut, the cloud began perceptibly to lift. A no-ball in the same over sent up the first ten.   Ten for two was not good; but it was considerably better than one for two.

With the score at thirty, Ellerby was missed in the slips off de Freece.   He had been playing with slowly increasing confidence till then, but this seemed to throw him out of his stride.   He played inside the next ball, and was all but bowled: and then, jumping out to drive, he was smartly stumped.   The cloud began to settle again.

Bob was the next man in.

Ellerby took off his pads, and dropped into the chair next to Mike's.   Mike was silent and thoughtful.   He was in after Bob, and to be on the eve of batting does not make one conversational.

"You in next?" asked Ellerby.

Mike nodded.

"It's getting trickier every minute," said Ellerby.   "The only thing is, if we can only stay in, we might have a chance. The wicket'll get better, and I don't believe they've any bowling at all bar de Freece.   By George, Bob's out! . . . No, he isn't."

Bob had jumped out at one of de Freece's slows, as

Ellerby had done, and had nearly met the same fate. The wicket-keeper, however, had fumbled the ball.

"That's the way I was had," said Ellerby. "That man's keeping such a jolly good length that you don't know whether to stay in your ground or go out at them. If only somebody would knock him off his length, I believe we might win yet."

The same idea apparently occurred to Burgess. He came to where Mike was sitting.

"I'm going to shove you down one, Jackson," he said. "I shall go in next myself and swipe, and try and knock that man de Freece off."

"All right," said Mike. He was not quite sure whether he was glad or sorry at the respite.

"It's a pity old Wyatt isn't here," said Ellerby. "This is just the sort of time when he might have come off."

"Bob's broken his egg," said Mike.

"Good man. Every little helps. . . . Oh, you silly ass, get *back*!"

Berridge had called Bob for a short run that was obviously no run. Third man was returning the ball as the batsmen crossed. The next moment the wicket-keeper had the bails off. Berridge was out by a yard.

"Forty-one for four," said Ellerby. "Help!"

Burgess began his campaign against de Freece by skying his first ball over cover's head to the boundary. A howl of delight went up from the school, which was repeated, *fortissimo*, when, more by accident than by accurate timing, the captain put on two more fours past extra-cover. The bowler's cheerful smile never varied.

Whether Burgess would have knocked de Freece off his length or not was a question that was destined to remain unsolved, for in the middle of the other bowler's over Bob hit a single; the batsmen crossed; and Burgess had his leg-stump uprooted while trying a gigantic pull-stroke.

The melancholy youth put up the figures, 54, 5, 12, on the board.

Mike, as he walked out of the pavilion to join Bob, was not conscious of any particular nervousness. It had been an ordeal having to wait and look on while wickets fell, but now that the time of inaction was at an end he felt curiously composed. When he had gone out to bat against the M.C.C. on the occasion of his first appearance for the school, he experienced a quaint sensation of unreality. He seemed to be watching his body walking to the wickets, as if it were someone else's. There was no sense of individuality.

But now his feelings were different. He was cool. He noticed small things—mid-off chewing bits of grass, the bowler re-tying the scarf round his waist, little patches of brown where the turf had been worn away. He took guard with a clear picture of the positions of the fieldsmen photographed on his brain.

Fitness, which in a batsman exhibits itself mainly in an increased power of seeing the ball, is one of the most inexplicable things connected with cricket. It has nothing, or very little, to do with actual health. A man may come out of a sick-room with just that extra quickness in sighting the ball that makes all the difference; or he may be in perfect training and play inside straight half-volleys. Mike would not have said that he felt more than ordinarily well that day. Indeed, he was rather painfully conscious of having bolted his food at lunch. But something seemed to whisper to him, as he settled himself to face the bowler, that he was at the top of his batting form. A difficult wicket always brought out his latent powers as a bat. It was a standing mystery with the sporting Press how Joe Jackson managed to collect fifties and sixties on wickets that completely upset men who were, apparently, finer players. On days when the Olympians of the cricket world were bringing their averages down with ducks and singles, Joe would be in his element, watching the ball and pushing it through the slips as if there were no such thing as a tricky wicket. And Mike took after Joe.

A single off the fifth ball of the over opened his score and brought him to the opposite end. Bob played ball number six back to the bowler, and Mike took guard preparatory to facing de Freece.

The Ripton slow bowler took a long run, considering his pace. In the early part of an innings he often trapped the batsmen in this way, by leading them to expect a faster ball than he actually sent down. A queer little jump in the middle of the run increased the difficulty of watching him.

The smiting he had received from Burgess in the previous over had not had the effect of knocking de Freece off his length. The ball was too short to reach with comfort, and not short enough to take liberties with. It pitched slightly to leg, and whipped in quickly. Mike had faced half-left, and stepped back. The increased speed of the ball after it had touched the ground beat him. The ball hit his right pad.

"'S that?" shouted mid-on. Mid-on has a habit of appealing for l.b.w. in school matches.

De Freece said nothing. The Ripton bowler was as conscientious in the matter of appeals as a good bowler should be. He had seen that the ball had pitched off the leg-stump.

The umpire shook his head. Mid-on tried to look as if he had not spoken.

Mike prepared himself for the next ball with a glow of confidence. He felt that he knew where he was now. Till then he had not thought the wicket was so fast. The two balls he had played at the other end had told him nothing. They had been well pitched up, and he had smothered them. He knew what to do now. He had played on wickets of this pace at home against Saunders' bowling, and Saunders had shown him the right way to cope with them.

The next ball was of the same length, but this time off the off-stump. Mike jumped out, and hit it before it had time to break. It flew along the ground through the gap between cover and extra-cover, a comfortable three.

Bob played out the over with elaborate care.

Off the second ball of the other man's over Mike scored his first boundary. It was a long-hop on the off. He banged it behind point to the terrace-bank. The last ball of the over, a half-volley to leg, he lifted over the other boundary.

"Sixty up," said Ellerby, in the pavilion, as the umpire signalled another no-ball. "By George! I believe these chaps are going to knock off the runs. Young Jackson looks as if he was in for a century."

"You ass," said Berridge. "Don't say that, or he's certain to get out."

Berridge was one of those who are skilled in cricket superstitions.

But Mike did not get out. He took seven off de Freece's next over by means of two cuts and a drive. And, with Bob still exhibiting a stolid and rock-like defence, the score mounted to eighty, thence to ninety, and so, mainly by singles, to a hundred.

At a hundred and four, when the wicket had put on exactly fifty, Bob fell to a combination of de Freece and extra-cover. He had stuck like a limpet for an hour and a quarter, and made twenty-one.

Mike watched him go with much the same feelings as those of a man who turns away from the platform after seeing a friend off on a long railway journey. His departure upset the scheme of things. For himself he had no fear now. He might possibly get out off his next ball, but he felt set enough to stay at the wickets till nightfall. He had had narrow escapes from de Freece, but he was full of that conviction, which comes to all batsmen on occasion, that this was his day. He had made twenty-six, and the wicket was getting easier. He could feel the sting going out of the bowling every over.

Henfrey, the next man in, was a promising rather than an effective bat. He had an excellent style, but he was uncertain. (Two years later, when he captained the Wrykyn teams, he made a lot of runs.)   But this season his batting had been spasmodic.

Today he never looked like settling down.   He survived an over from de Freece, and hit a fast change bowler who had been put on at the other end for a couple of fluky fours. Then Mike got the bowling for three consecutive overs, and raised the score to a hundred and twenty-six.   A bye brought Henfrey to the batting end again, and de Freece's pet googly, which had not been much in evidence hitherto, led to his snicking an easy catch into short-slip's hands.

A hundred and twenty-seven for seven against a total of a hundred and sixty-six gives the impression that the batting side has the advantage.   In the present case, however, it was Ripton who were really in the better position.   Apparently, Wrykyn had three more wickets to fall.   Practically they had only one, for neither Ashe, nor Grant, nor Devenish had any pretensions to be considered batsmen.   Ashe was the school wicket-keeper.   Grant and Devenish were bowlers.   Between them the three could not be relied on for a dozen in a decent match.

Mike watched Ashe shape with a sinking heart.   The wicket-keeper looked like a man who feels that his hour has come.   Mike could see him licking his lips.   There was nervousness written all over him.

He was not kept long in suspense.   De Freece's first ball made a hideous wreck of his wicket.

"Over," said the umpire.

Mike felt that the school's one chance now lay in his keeping the bowling.   But how was he to do this?   It suddenly occurred to him that it was a delicate position that he was in.   It was not often that he was troubled by an inconvenient modesty, but this happened now.   Grant was a fellow he hardly knew, and a school prefect to boot.   Could he go up to him and explain that he, Jackson, did not consider him competent to bat in this crisis?   Would not this get about and be accounted to him for side?   He had made forty, but even so . . .

Fortunately Grant solved the problem on his own account. He came up to Mike and spoke with an earnestness born of nerves. "For goodness' sake," he whispered, "collar the bowling all you know, or we're done. I shall get outed first ball."

"All right," said Mike, and set his teeth. Forty to win! A large order. But it was going to be done. His whole existence seemed to concentrate itself on those forty runs.

The fast bowler, who was the last of several changes that had been tried at the other end, was well meaning but erratic. The wicket was almost true again now, and it was possible to take liberties.

Mike took them.

A distant clapping from the pavilion, taken up a moment later all round the ground, and echoed by the Ripton fieldsmen, announced that he had reached his fifty.

The last ball of the over he mishit. It rolled in the direction of third man.

"Co e on," shouted Grant.

Mike and the ball arrived at the opposite wicket almost simultaneously. Another fraction of a second, and he would have been run out.

The last balls of the next two overs provided repetitions of this performance. But each time luck was with him, and his bat was across the crease before the bails were off. The telegraph-board showed a hundred and fifty.

The next over was doubly sensational. The original medium-paced bowler had gone on again in place of the fast man, and for the first five balls he could not find his length. During those five balls Mike raised the score to a hundred and sixty.

But the sixth was of a different kind. Faster than the rest and of a perfect length, it all but got through Mike's defence. As it was, he stopped it. But he did not score. The umpire called "Over!" and there was Grant at the batting end, with de Freece smiling pleasantly as he walked back to begin his run with the comfortable reflection that at last he had got somebody except Mike to bowl at.

That over was an experience Mike never forgot.

Grant pursued the Fabian policy of keeping his bat almost immovable and trusting to luck. Point and the slips crowded round. Mid-off and mid-on moved half-way down the pitch. Grant looked embarrassed, but determined. For four balls he baffled the attack, though once nearly caught by point a yard from the wicket. The fifth curled round his bat, and touched the off-stump. A bail fell silently to the ground.

Devenish came in to take the last ball of the over.

It was an awe-inspiring moment. A great stillness was over all the ground. Mike's knees trembled. Devenish's face was a delicate grey.

The only person unmoved seemed to be de Freece. His smile was even more amiable than usual as he began his run.

The next moment the crisis was past. The ball hit the very centre of Devenish's bat, and rolled back down the pitch.

The school broke into one great howl of joy. There were still seven runs between them and victory, but nobody appeared to recognize this fact as important. Mike had got the bowling, and the bowling was not de Freece's.

It seemed almost an anti-climax when a four to leg and two two's through the slips settled the thing.

Devenish was caught and bowled in de Freece's next over; but the Wrykyn total was one hundred and seventy-two.

.   .   .   .   .

"Good game," said Maclaine, meeting Burgess in the pavilion. "Who was the man who made all the runs? How many, by the way?"

"Eighty-three. It was young Jackson. Brother of the other one."

"*That* family! How many more of them are you going to have here?"

"He's the last. I say, rough luck on de Freece. He bowled magnificently."

Politeness to a beaten foe caused Burgess to change his usual "not bad."

"The funny part of it is," continued he, "that young Jackson was only playing as a sub."

"You've got a rum idea of what's funny," said Maclaine.

CHAPTER XXIX

WYATT AGAIN

IT was a morning in the middle of September. The Jacksons were breakfasting. Mr. Jackson was reading letters. The rest, including Gladys Maud, whose finely-chiselled features were gradually disappearing behind a mask of bread-and-milk, had settled down to serious work. The usual catch-as-catch-can contest between Marjory and Phyllis for the jam (referee and time-keeper, Mrs. Jackson) had resulted, after both combatants had been cautioned by the referee, in a victory for Marjory, who had duly secured the stakes. The hour being nine-fifteen, and the official time for breakfast nine o'clock, Mike's place was still empty.

"I've had a letter from MacPherson," said Mr. Jackson.

MacPherson was the vigorous and persevering gentleman, referred to in a previous chapter, who kept a fatherly eye on the Buenos Aires sheep.

"He seems very satisfied with Mike's friend Wyatt. At the moment of writing Wyatt is apparently incapacitated owing to a bullet in the shoulder, but expects to be fit again shortly. That young man seems to make things fairly lively wherever he is. I don't wonder he found a public school too restricted a sphere for his energies."

"Has he been fighting a duel?" asked Marjory, interested.

"Bushrangers," said Phyllis.

"There aren't any bushrangers in Buenos Aires," said Ella.

"How do you know?" said Phyllis clinchingly.

"Bush-ray, bush-ray, bush-ray," began Gladys Maud,

conversationally, through the bread-and-milk; but was headed off.

"He gives no details. Perhaps that letter on Mike's plate supplies them. I see it comes from Buenos Aires."

"I wish Mike would come and open it," said Marjory. "Shall I go and hurry him up?"

The missing member of the family entered as she spoke.

"Buck up, Mike," she shouted. "There's a letter from Wyatt. He's been wounded in a duel."

"With a bushranger," added Phyllis.

"Bush-ray," explained Gladys Maud.

"Is there?" said Mike. "Sorry I'm late."

He opened the letter and began to read.

"What does he say?" inquired Marjory. "Who was the duel with?"

"How many bushrangers were there?" asked Phyllis.

Mike read on.

"Good old Wyatt! He's shot a man."

"Killed him?" asked Marjory excitedly.

"No. Only potted him in the leg. This is what he says. First page is mostly about the Ripton match and so on. Here you are. 'I'm dictating this to a sportsman of the name of Danvers, a good chap who can't help being ugly, so excuse bad writing. The fact is we've been having a bust-up here, and I've come out of it with a bullet in the shoulder, which has crocked me for the time being. It happened like this. An ass of a Gaucho had gone into the town and got jolly tight, and coming back, he wanted to ride through our place. The old woman who keeps the lodge wouldn't have it at any price. So this rotter, instead of shifting off, proceeded to cut the fence, and go through that way. All the farms out here have their boundaries marked by wire fences, and it is supposed to be a deadly sin to cut these. Well, the lodge-keeper's son dashed off in search of help. A chap called Chester, an Old Wykehamist, and I were dipping sheep close by, so he came to us and told us what had happened. We nipped on to a couple of horses, pulled out our revolvers, and tooled after him. After a bit we overtook him, and that's when the trouble began. The johnny had dismounted when we arrived. I thought he was simply tightening his horse's girths. What he was really doing was getting a steady aim at us with his revolver. He fired as we came up, and dropped poor old Chester. I thought he was killed at first, but it turned out it was only his leg. I got going then. I emptied all the six chambers of my revolver, and missed him clean every time. In the meantime he got me in the right shoulder. Hurt like sin afterwards, though it was only a sort of dull shock at the moment. The next item of the programme was a forward move in force on the part of the enemy. The man had got his knife out now—why he didn't shoot again I don't know—and toddled over in our direction to finish us off. Chester was unconscious, and it was any money on the Gaucho, when I happened to catch sight of Chester's pistol, which had fallen just by where I came down. I picked it up, and loosed off. Missed the first shot, but got him with the second in the ankle at about two yards; and *his* day's work was done. That's the painful story. Danvers says he's getting writer's cramp, so I shall have to stop....'"

"By Jove!" said Mike.

"What a dreadful thing!" said Mrs. Jackson.

"Anyhow, it was practically a bushranger," said Phyllis.

"I told you it was a duel, and so it was," said Marjory.

"What a terrible experience for the poor boy!" said Mrs. Jackson.

"Much better than being in a beastly bank," said Mike, summing up. "I'm glad he's having such a ripping time. It must be almost as decent as Wrykyn out there.... I say, what's under that dish?"

FOR THE BEST IN PAPERBACKS, LOOK FOR THE

In every corner of the world, on every subject under the sun, Penguin represents quality and variety – the very best in publishing today.

For complete information about books available from Penguin – including Puffins, Penguin Classics and Arkana – and how to order them, write to us at the appropriate address below. Please note that for copyright reasons the selection of books varies from country to country.

In the United Kingdom: Please write to *Dept E.P., Penguin Books Ltd, Harmondsworth, Middlesex, UB7 0DA.*

If you have any difficulty in obtaining a title, please send your order with the correct money, plus ten per cent for postage and packaging, to *PO Box No 11, West Drayton, Middlesex*

In the United States: Please write to *Dept BA, Penguin, 299 Murray Hill Parkway, East Rutherford, New Jersey 07073*

In Canada: Please write to *Penguin Books Canada Ltd, 2801 John Street, Markham, Ontario L3R 1B4*

In Australia: Please write to the *Marketing Department, Penguin Books Australia Ltd, P.O. Box 257, Ringwood, Victoria 3134*

In New Zealand: Please write to the *Marketing Department, Penguin Books (NZ) Ltd, Private Bag, Takapuna, Auckland 9*

In India: Please write to *Penguin Overseas Ltd, 706 Eros Apartments, 56 Nehru Place, New Delhi, 110019*

In the Netherlands: Please write to *Penguin Books Netherlands B.V., Postbus 195, NL–1380AD Weesp*

In West Germany: Please write to *Penguin Books Ltd, Friedrichstrasse 10–12, D–6000 Frankfurt/Main 1*

In Spain: Please write to *Longman Penguin España, Calle San Nicolas 15, E–28013 Madrid*

In Italy: Please write to *Penguin Italia s.r.l., Via Como 4, I-20096 Pioltello (Milano)*

In France: Please write to *Penguin Books Ltd, 39 Rue de Montmorency, F-75003 Paris*

In Japan: Please write to *Longman Penguin Japan Co Ltd, Yamaguchi Building, 2–12–9 Kanda Jimbocho, Chiyoda-Ku, Tokyo 101*

THE ADVENTURES OF MIKE AND PSMITH

Mike and Psmith

It was a preference for cricket over schoolwork that caused Mike to be removed from Wrykyn and Psmith from Eton. But Sedleigh is sorely unprepared for boys of their resources and foresight. The school, as Psmith would say, confuses the unusual with the impossible, and is thus taken very much by surprise by the duo in their element.

Psmith in the City

Psmith and his friend Mike are sent by their fathers to work in the City – but the ponderous ritual of a mere bank cannot dent Psmith's flippant irresponsibility. A battle of wits develops, and wit has always been Psmith's sharpest weapon ...

Leave it to Psmith

Psmith goes to Blandings, where he bemuses Lord Emsworth, embroils Beach, enrages Baxter and enslaves Miss Halliday. But, with his usual aplomb, he brings everything to a satisfactory conclusion, except perhaps for Freddie Threepwood.

Psmith, Journalist

The New York magazine *Cosy Moments* did not have a reputation for controversy – until Psmith allowed his literary aspirations to run riot. Soon he and his friend Billy are chased by gangsters, and life is certainly not cosy any more.